THE LAND OF NO HORIZONS

By Alan Benson

Order this book online at www.trafford.com/08-1054
or email orders@trafford.com

Most Trafford titles are also available at major online book retailers.

© Copyright 2009 Alan Benson.

All rights reserved. No part of this publication may be reproduced, stored in a retrieval system, or transmitted, in any form or by any means, electronic, mechanical, photocopying, recording, or otherwise, without the written prior permission of the author.

Note for Librarians: A cataloguing record for this book is available from Library and Archives Canada at www.collectionscanada.ca/amicus/index-e.html

Printed in Victoria, BC, Canada.

ISBN: 978-1-4251-8549-7

We at Trafford believe that it is the responsibility of us all, as both individuals and corporations, to make choices that are environmentally and socially sound. You, in turn, are supporting this responsible conduct each time you purchase a Trafford book, or make use of our publishing services. To find out how you are helping, please visit www.trafford.com/responsiblepublishing.html

Our mission is to efficiently provide the world's finest, most comprehensive book publishing service, enabling every author to experience success. To find out how to publish your book, your way, and have it available worldwide, visit us online at www.trafford.com/10510

www.trafford.com

North America & international
toll-free: 1 888 232 4444 (USA & Canada)
phone: 250 383 6864 ♦ fax: 250 383 6804
email: info@trafford.com

The United Kingdom & Europe
phone: +44 (0)1865 487 395 ♦ local rate: 0845 230 9601
facsimile: +44 (0)1865 481 507 ♦ email: info.uk@trafford.com

10 9 8 7 6 5 4 3 2

The land of no horizons

I would like to thank
my editing team without
there help this book would never
have happened.

Special thanks to my brother Norman
and my wife Linda.

The land of no horizons

CHAPTER ONE

The pain in his fingers was excruciating, his muscles burned from the relentless pressure he put on them, he didn't know how much longer he could hold on. His toes were also starting to hurt and he wasn't sure that they wouldn't give way! He didn't want to think about that. This looked like an easy climb when they started and so it was, until now. This was a very difficult spot, one of the worst he'd ever been in. He tried to block the pain from his mind as he'd done so many times before.

There was a small finger hold about six inches higher up but he had no idea of how deep it

The land of no horizons

was. Could he get his fingers in there and if he did, was it deep enough to give him a good grip, his and another life might depend on it?

"There's a toe hold about three inches up from your left foot, it's about four inches to your left," the familiar voice of his brother said.

"Ok, that might help. Are we secure, this next bit looks bloody dangerous? If I don't make it I hope those anchors work because if they don't it's a long way down."

"*We're* good, if you think you can make it, then go for it and don't worry I won't let you fall, well not far anyway."

"That sounds reassuring. This is turning out to be one of the toughest climbs yet," Russell said.

"Once we get up a bit higher things seem to get a little easier, there's a large crack in the rock face, when you get there you should have lots to hang onto," Stuart said.

"I hope you're right, because from here it looks very difficult."

Russ steadied himself, he reached for the small toe hold that Stuart had told him about, it was

The land of no horizons

a good one, at least two inches deep and wide enough to get all his toes in. This was not a very big platform to do what he had to do next. He closed his eyes took two deep breaths letting each one out slowly. Then he opened his eyes and concentrated on his next move.

Focusing all his strength in his toes and legs he powered himself upwards towards the hand grip he hoped was there. The fingers of his right hand penetrated the bottom of the crack that split the rock face. His fingers held as he swung a thousand feet from the ground below. His left hand was grasping, scraping for a small depression or something other than the smooth rock face. At first it seemed hopeless then he found a small depression for his left hand. Next his left foot found a tiny crack in the rock face and his right foot found it also.

Russell thought he could see a small crack over to his left so he reached up again and managed to slip a couple of fingers into it. Finding that small finger hole gave him confidence, he gripped just as hard as he could. Now with both hands secure he breathed again. Pressing his toes into the small

The land of no horizons

crack in the rock, he managed to get a little traction, then he struggled to pushed himself up a bit more. His right hand now moved to a slightly better grip, followed by his left hand which also found a better finger hole.

It was about ten minutes later that he finally felt that he was in a good place and now he could rest a little.

"You had me worried there for a minute Russ, I thought this one was going to be too much for you."

"This is almost as bad as the one in the Alps, we did two years ago. Do you remember that one?"

"I'll never forget that place, I thought we were both dead that day."

After a short breather Russ started off again, slowly, inch by inch, foot by foot, he climbed that rock wall with Stuart following a short distance behind.

It took nearly two hours to climb the last fifty feet or so. That only got them to a small ledge. The ledge was about eighteen inches wide, and three feet long. But it was large enough to sit on and enjoy the

The land of no horizons

view.

They opened their knapsacks, took out their sandwiches and ate ravenously. Washing their food down with bottles of cold water.

The view from up here was spectacular, they could see the road that had brought them here. A few cars drove along not knowing they were being watched. The sun was very warm but up here in the Rocky Mountains there's always a cool breeze.

This was vacation time for the Barron brothers and this was one of their favorite ways to spend it. Russ loved to climb and Stuart went along just to keep an eye on his older brother.

Russ was the older of the two, but only by eight minutes. Most people didn't believe that they were brothers never mind twins. So many times they had to produce drivers' licences, or passport just to appease people they hardly knew. But over the years they had grown accustomed to the problems of being fraternal twins, instead of identical ones.

Now they were here on vacation. They had both taken the whole month of August off, with no set plan of where to go. No timetable was a one of

The land of no horizons

their favorite ways to vacation. They had packed a couple of suitcases, their knapsacks, all their climbing and pot holing gear and headed north.

They left California passed through Oregon and spent a night in Seattle. The next day they left early trying to get into the Rocky's by early afternoon. Their hotel was just off the Interstate 5, so around four thirty they drove onto the I-5, and headed north. When they got to Highway 20, they left the I-5 and headed towards the Cascade Mountain range. They stayed on I-20 until they hit the 97 heading north. This road took them up to the Canadian border. They crossed the border into Canada heading for the Rocky mountains.

They always took Stuart's SUV on holiday with them, his top of the line Lincoln Navigator was better suited to what they liked to do than was Russell's Porsche Boxster. It took the Mountain roads easily and it had lots of room for backpacks tents and camping gear.

Three and a half hours after crossing into

The land of no horizons
British Columbia they were heading north towards Radium Hot Springs, having left Cranbrook and Kimberly behind them.

They spotted this rock face from a couple of miles away. It didn't look too easy, or too difficult for their first climb in almost a year.

They parked the Navigator and walked for about half an hour to reach the base of the face. Four hours later they were siting on a small ledge looking out on the world. They were very satisfied with the climb, it was just what they needed to get their vacation going.

"Where do you feel like going to now that we are finally away from work?" Stuart asked.

"I haven't got the slightest idea, is there anywhere you would like to go?"

"I was just thinking about that, but I don't seem to be able to think of anywhere that we haven't already been too."

"It's difficult when you've traveled as much as we have, there aren't many places we haven't been too at least once." Russ said.

"There's one thing I've been wanting to do for

The land of no horizons

a long time now that we haven't done. We haven't seen a volcano up close"

"That's true, but where would you like to go?"

"Mount Etna in Italy is having one of her biggest rumblings in years, the papers were saying. And we haven't been to Italy for at least six years."

Russ thought for a minute then he shrugged his shoulders and said, "that sounds like a great idea, lets go to Italy."

"Which is the best way to get there from here?"

"I don't know, but usually getting there is half the fun."

The land of no horizons

CHAPTER TWO

It had taken five days to get from that ledge in the Rocky's to Rome's Leonardo da Vinci Airport. The airport is a modern building, bustling with excited people going on holidays, or meeting family or friends coming back from exotic places. *Airports are a great place to people watch,* Stuart thought. *Especially in foreign country's where the customs are so different from our own.*

When they climbed down from that cliff face they took a scenic drive through the rocky's, stopping to do a little sightseeing along the way. It's hard to drive past places like Banff and Lake Louise without stopping for a few hours. They both agreed that Lake Louise was

The land of no horizons

a very beautiful place.

This was not the first time they had been to the lake. When they were kid's their parents rented a motor home and they drove through this part of Canada. It was one of those great family times that kids remember. It was probably that holiday that started the boy's interest in the great outdoors.

They did for the first time, some of the things that they now love to do. Rock climbing, fishing, camping, just enjoying being outside, away from the big cities. That holiday was full of fond memories. It was a great family holiday probably the best one they ever had.

Because their dad is a workaholic, he doesn't like to take time off for holidays. The only time he's really happy is when he's at work. When they were young vacation time was usually spent with mum. They traveled a lot but for two young boys it was not the same without dad. They never complained they just silently wished that dad could come along too.

The land of no horizons

When they arrived in Calgary, they put the Navigator in long term parking and caught a plane for London, England.

There were no flights directly to Rome so London seemed the most logical place to go. They only planned to stay overnight, but they ended up staying for three days. Besides climbing mountains, the brothers liked to have a good time, and London is one of the world's great cities for that.

The Barron brothers had been to London many times and they knew the city well. The nightlife in London is second to none, if you know where to look, and they know where all the top clubs are. Most of the best clubs are in the Knights Bridge area or around Mayfair.

To get into these clubs you have to pay an exorbitant membership fee. Or you have to pay an even more exorbitant door charge. The only way around these fees' is to go in with a member. This was a great reason to connect with some old friends who they hadn't seen in years.

Russ and Stuart had no problems fitting in with these people. Back home they would often be

The land of no horizons

asked to come out and play with the rich and famous. That was the lifestyle that they had grown up in and were comfortable with.

It was their parents who introduced them into the good life, the life that money and success can bring. Their mother especially liked to hobnob with wealthy people. She was herself a movie star at one time. Until she met Lawrence J Barron. The handsome son of J. J. Barron, president of Barron Pharmaceuticals.

Lawrence with his charm and his style, swept her off her feet. They fell in love and were married just a few short months' later.

Veronica Chapel was their mother's stage name and she liked to use it when she was around her Hollywood friends, which she still had lots of. The Barron family was well known around Hollywood because they would occasionally invest some money in a movie, or even a TV show. The boys thought this was done just so mom could hang around with actors and directors, more than for any profit they made from their investments. But it kept mom happy and when mom was happy, dad was

The land of no horizons

happy.

Mom had acted in a few movies. She had a staring roll in two B type movies. Her most famous one was a horror movie, one of those where young couples are killed off all through the show. In the one mom was in, she was the last one to die. But when she died she was naked. So the boys have never been allowed to seen it.

Dad is totally different from mom, he was very ambitious. He was very hard working and a very quiet man. He chose his words well and when he spoke people listened.

It was *his* father, that had started Barron Pharmaceuticals, back in the nineteen twenties. But it was Lawrence that had taken the company from a small business of thirteen people, to a multinational conglomerate employing thousands of people in six different countries.

Barron Pharmaceuticals is not one of those companies that makes drugs. It makes and distributes the small things that all hospitals, clinics, and doctors offices can't manage without. They make syringes in China, and distribute them around

The land of no horizons

the world. They make heart catheters, that are used in many modern heart operations. They have also expanded into the larger computer operated diagnostic machines, that hospitals pay tens of thousands of dollars for.

This is where the future growth for our company is, Lawrence would say and nobody would disagree with him.

Both the boys held executive positions in the company. Stuart was in charge of distribution. While Russell was in charge of new product development. The boys hated the fact that they got their jobs because of their dad and not on their own merits. This meant that they had to work twice as hard as anyone else in the company, or they wouldn't get any respect from the other executives. Dad had also told them, that he would fire their ass's out of there, if they let him or the company down. And he meant it.

Stuart used his credit card to rent a convertible Mercedes Benz at the airport. It was very hot day as

The land of no horizons

they drove south out of Rome heading towards Sicily.

It was a little after one o'clock when they left Rome behind. Without a care in the world the boys sped down the road feeling like they were finally on vacation. California seemed a long way away and so did work with all the pressures that go with it.

The Autostrade is an excellent road smooth and fast like some American Highways. Their plans were very simple, drive down to Naples and from there catch a ferry to Sicily. They didn't care where in Sicily they went to, it's not a big island and a big volcano shouldn't be hard to find.

As the Mercedes sped smoothly down the highway, the twins couldn't have been happier. Down the road a little way they could see two girls hitch hiking, one had a sign that said *Sicilia,* which the boys knew was what the Italians called Sicily. Stuart put the brakes on hard and stopped about a hundred yards ahead of the girls.

The girls came running down the hard shoulder towards the car. As they got close, they slowed down, when they saw the boys they seemed

The land of no horizons

a little hesitant.

"We are going all the way to Sicily, if you want a ride?" Russell said.

The two girls looked at them and they seemed very unsure. Their eyes flashed back and forth and they whispered to each other.

Stuart looked over and gave them a big comforting smile and said, " we are going to Sicily and if you want a ride you can sure have one, or if you want, you can wait for another car to stop?"

"Are you going to Sicily even if we don't get in the car," one of the girls asked, in a very pleasant English accent?

"Yes, we're going to see Mt Etna while she's erupting," Russ said.

"Ok, if we come with you, we ride in the back and you stay in the front," the dark-haired girl said, in good English but with an Italian accent.

"Get in girls, you'll be safe with us don't worry," Russ said as he opened the back door and the girls slid onto the back seat.

The land of no horizons

"I'm Stuart and this is my brother Russ, what are your names?"

"I'm Sondra and this is my best friend Capena," the girl with the English accent said.

"Nice to meet you girls," Stuart said as he shook their hands. "Are you going to Sicily for a holiday?"

"No, I live there," Capena said.

"*You live there*, that's great, maybe you can help us find a back way up the mountain? Somewhere away from the tourists," Russ said.

"I can do that, my father knows the mountain better than anyone else on the island."

"That's fantastic, it was lucky for us that we ran into you girls like that," Stuart said.

"Where are you girls coming from?" Russell asked.

"We are at collage. We go to a small collage near Oxford," Sondra said. "We're just starting our summer holidays."

"We're just starting our vacation too," Stuart said. "Is there anything worth seeing in Sicily besides the mountain."

The land of no horizons

"Oh yes, there are lots of places worth seeing. It's only a small island but it is very pretty this time of year," Copena replied.

"I bet there are some great places to eat?" Stuart said.

"All you think about is your stomach, you will have to wait for a while," Russell said.

"But I'm hungry, we only had airline food and you know how I hate that stuff."

"Hopefully you girls will show us around while we are here," Russell said, ignoring his brother.

"I would like that," Copena said. "How long do you think you will be staying on the island?"

"Not long, three maybe four days." Russell replied.

The girls seemed to relax a little, when they realized that the boys were genuine and meant them no harm.

Sondra was from London and she was very chatty. With that very English accent it was a pleasure to listen to her talk.

Capena was very pretty with dark hair and

The land of no horizons

beautiful dark eyes. She was slim with long legs that were very tanned. Sondra was the opposite she had dirty blond hair and blue eyes, a very fair skin, she was slim also. She wasn't bad looking, but she didn't have the sultry good looks that her friend had.

"We were going to go to Naples and catch a ferry from there to the island, what do you think is best?" Stuart said.

"That's the quickest way but it is also the most expensive way, we were going to Reggio di Calabria, the ferry is much cheaper from there," Copena said.

"We are not too worried about the cost, if we pay for you, will you stay with us? You can be a big help," Russ said.

"Ok by me," Sondra said.

"If that's ok with you, Copena?" Russ asked.

"Yes, I guess so," she replied.

The land of no horizons

CHAPTER THREE

The drive was leisurely, the weather was perfect and the girls were great company. They were full of stories about life at a British University. The drinking, the parties the fun times. Also all the hard work that they had to do. The university that they were at was a girls only school, not as big as some of the other more famous collages in Oxford.

The whole town of Oxford seemed to be there just for students and the students took full advantage of it.

The college's that the boys went to were very similar, lots of partying and then lots of cramming just before the big tests.

The land of no horizons

The Mercedes was a dream to drive it handled the road without any problems at all. This part of Italy was very changeable, they drove through countryside, then into a small town. They would see the Tyrrhenian Sea, then they would be back amongst the houses again. The brothers loved to drive and this was just as they liked it, nice scenery, nice company, good weather and a great car. Capena pointed out places of interest along the way, it was like having a tour guide with them.

After a short stop at a pizza restaurant, they did the last few miles to the ferry. It was just after seven thirty when they got there and the next ferry was at eight. The four of them just sat in the car waiting their turn to get on the boat.

It was dark when they drove off the ferry and into Palermo. The boys were surprised by Palermo, it was not the little tiny fishing village that they had expected. The city was a modern urban area, with all the attributes of a large city. In most parts the roads were wide and there was an extensive Highway system.

The land of no horizons

The drive out to Capena's parents place took them through the city and out to the hillsides overlooking the city of Palermo. And although they were quite a distance from the volcano they could smell the sulphur in the air and sometimes in the distance they could see a dark red glow in the distant night sky.

Copena had told them many stories about Mt Etna, about how her father had lived all his life in the shadow of this great mountain. Stories about people dying and about people going missing, never to be seen again. There had been lots of eruptions over the years. Most of which were just minor ones but there were stories of big ones, with massive larva flows that nothing could stop.

The locals seemed to give the mountain a lot of respect. This didn't change the boy's minds, it only made them more anxious to climb it and see what secrets it had to show them.

Where Copina's family lived was like something out of a tourist guide book. It was only a small house built into the rock face of a hillside, it was not attached to the houses on either side but it

The land of no horizons

was so close that it was impossible to get between them.

As the car pulled up outside the house, the front door opened and people started to flood out onto the front yard. Capena jumped out of the car and was immediately mobbed by her family. The scene was as it should be, the daughter coming home from school and everyone overjoyed to see her.

Sondra and the boys slowly climbed out of the Mercades, leaned against the car and waited for the celebration to die down a little.

After a couple of minutes Copena came down the small path dragging a man and a woman with her. "Mama, papa, these are my friends this is Sondra and these two are Russell and Stuart," she said.

"It is nice to meet you," the man said in good English but with a very strong Italian accent.

"It's nice to meet you to sir," Russ said as he shook his hand.

"Me to," Stuart said, as he shook the man's hand.

The land of no horizons

"We were expecting you Sondra, but not the two gentlemen," Copena's dad said. "But you are all very welcome, please come in and we shall share some wine with our new friends."

Everyone headed into the little house. The excitement was overwhelming, everyone was buzzing around Copena asking question after question. She looked to be coping well, talking to everyone in turn trying not to miss anyone. Sondra was beside Copena soaking up the atmosphere, joining in when she could. The boys just stood at one side not saying anything just watching everyone have fun.

In the midst of the commotion the father came over and quietly took the boys into the kitchen.

"That is for the women," he said pointing to the other room, "we men will sit in here and drink a little wine like men are supposed to do."

"It is noisy in there" Russ said.

"Huh, huh," he said, "please sit down and I will find us some good wine."

The table that they sat down at looked very old, the top was one solid piece of wood that had

The land of no horizons

been washed so many times that it wasn't flat anymore. The chairs looked like someone who didn't have much carpentry skills had put them together. But they seemed to match the table perfectly.

Copena's father was a tall man over six feet tall and he walked with his back straight as if he had been in the army for many years. He disappeared into another room and was gone for a moment or two.

Looking around the room it was obvious that this was not a rich household. There was very little furniture in either room that they had been in and the furniture that there was, looked to be homemade. This room, beside the table and four chairs, had only a cupboard with a glassed in portion on the top.

Soon he returned with a bottle of wine and three glasses. Gently placing the wine and the glasses on the table, he said "how long have you known my daughter?"

"We only met her this afternoon. They were looking for a ride and we were coming to Sicily anyway. So we asked them, to come along with us.

The land of no horizons

That way they could help us with the language, as we don't speak any Italian," Stuart said.

"And why were you coming here?"

"We want to go up the volcano, if we can," Russ said.

"The mountain is not a good place to be," Copena's dad said. "The ground is shaking all the time she is getting ready for a large eruption. The experts say it will not happen but I believe it will and soon."

"Your daughter says you know the mountain better than anyone around here," Russell said.

"It is true, I have lived here all my life. I have given tours of the mountain. And for many years I was the head of the search and rescue team for this area. The mountain is in my blood and she has some of mine in her."

At this point he pulled the cork from the wine bottle and filled the three glasses to the brim. He picked up his glass and took a sip. "That is good," he said, "please, try some."

Both boys carefully picked up a glass and took a sip.

The land of no horizons

"That's very good," Stuart said.

"Tell me sir..." Russ started to say.

"Please don't call me sir, my name is Elondro, please call me that."

"Ok, Elondro, what I was going to ask you is, can you tell us a way to get up the mountain, also we would like to stay away from the tourists, if we can?" Russ said.

"There are not too many tourists when the mountain is as active as she is. The guides will not take people up it's too dangerous. I have a map and I can show you a good way to get close to the top but you must be very carful. This mountain has taken lots of lives. This back way up the mountain is not an easy way. If you are not experienced climber's, then I don't think you can make it."

"We have done lots of climbing, we have climbed mountains in the Rocky's and the Alps," Stuart said.

Elondro climbed out of his chair with some difficulty and he walked over to the cupboard, he opened one of the drawers. He pulled out a large piece of paper that was rolled up to form a tube. He

The land of no horizons

gave the boys a smile as he brought it back to the table. There he unrolled it onto the table.

The map was almost as big as the top of the table. So both boys stood up so that they could see it better. The map was of the whole island. But this was not a tourist map, it was a very detailed map full of all kinds of information. All the distances were in meters and kilometers and all the writing was in Italian. As the boys looked at it closely, they had no problems understanding it.

"This is where we are," Elondro said pointing to Palermo on the map. "If you take this road that leads south-west out of town, about three miles down this road there is a small road off to your right." He pointed to the spot on the map. "Most people don't notice it because it is behind a closed gate, but the gate is never locked. This road goes all the way around the bottom of the mountain and goes onto Syracuse. But just before that there is a dirt road, that is also well hidden, that goes almost half way up the mountain. It is not a good road but you can get a long way up that way. The problem is that in 1988 the lava flow crossed the road and now you

The land of no horizons

have a long climb to get past it".

"Once you have crossed the lava, it is a difficult walk to the top. Of course you can't get close to the top when she is active like she is. It is much too dangerous to get within half a mile from the crater. Plus the heat and the fumes, won't let you get close."

"You have picked a bad time to come here, when she is so angry, like she is now, it is not safe to climb her. The experts say that she is going to have a major eruption within the next few months, I think it will be in the next few weeks and possibly the next few days. If you do go up there be very careful, the conditions can change very quickly, on Etna."

The boys had been listening very intently to what he had been saying to them. "Thank's Elondro, we will take great care when we do this, what you have told us is very helpful," Russ said as he took a closer look at the map.

At that moment Copena's mother came in and shouted something in Italian at Elondro. "I have to put the map away, she says that I have to join the

The land of no horizons

rest of the party in the other room. But if you want, I will leave it out and you two can have another look at it?"

"If you could leave it out, we will put it away when we've finished with it," Stuart said.

Elondro gave them a big smile, picked up his glass of wine and went to join the others in the front room.

The land of no horizons

CHAPTER FOUR

It was a dog barking not too far away that woke Stuart up. There was a nice warm breeze blowing in off the water. He blinked a couple of times and tried to turn over but a shooting pain in his back prevented that.

Where the hell am I? he thought. Then slowly he started to remember the night before. How after Elondro went back to the party, he and Russell studied the map some more. Russ then found a pen and paper and did a quick copy of the map.

Then they replaced the map in the drawer and joined the party themselves.

The wine flowed freely, a little too freely. By the time the boys left the party they were both too

The land of no horizons

drunk to drive, so they decided to sleep in the car. They tossed a coin and of course Russ won. That's why Stuart's in the front seat with a terrible pain in his back and Russ is sleeping like a baby in the back.

Stuart looked out of the car. The sun was high up in the sky. The houses all looked different in the light of day. The road was very narrow where the car was parked, hardly enough room to get another car passed.

Capenas house was quiet, as were all the other houses around there. The only other noise, *besides the barking dog*, was Russ snoring in the back seat.

"Wake up Russ you lazy ass. Its after ten and we should be on the road already."

Russ didn't move. "Wake up now or I will throw cold water on you," Stuart said. There was a slight groaning sound and then the sound of sticky flesh on leather seats.

"I think I drank too much last night, I feel like crap," Russell said.

"And so you should, you made a fool out of yourself last night, drinking as much as you did."

The land of no horizons

"I didn't do anything stupid did I?"

"*No*, not unless you call serenading Copenas mother something stupid."

"*Please,* tell me I didn't."

"Oh yes you did, and you were singing in Italian too."

"But I don't know any Italian," Russ said.

"That was obvious from your singing."

Russ climbed into the front seat and said, "I *need* coffee and lots of it."

"Ok, lets go into town and see what we can find."

It was shortly after noon and the Mercedes was moving along smoothly down the winding country road. Stuart was driving, not too fast because they had twice suddenly come across sheep in the middle of the road.

Alondro had told them there was a road, that was hard to see, because there was a gate blocking the way.

Stuart, drove past the road before he saw it. Then he had to back up, so that Russ could jump out

The land of no horizons

and open the gate. Now the road was much different. This road was in very bad condition, if it was a proper road. The pot holes were huge and some parts the road had been washed away completely.

They drove on for about five miles and then they started down a dirt road, all the time getting closer to the mountain. The dirt road was slowly climbing up a hillside. When they reached the top of one small hill, there was Etna, large and angry looking, spiting out smoke and dust.

"Oh my god," Russ said, " she looks different from this angle. She looks *I don't know the right words for her*, she looks impressive."

"She is all that and more. I hope this road goes up a long way or we will have a long walk when we get out."

"It's a good job we brought all our hiking gear with us, just in case we have to spend the night on the mountain," Russ said.

"Lets try and not spend the night if we can, we did promise Copena that we would go to their house tonight, for the proper party. Remember?"

"Er, no, I don't remember that. Did you

The land of no horizons

promise we would go?"

"No you did. Just after you drank the wine out of that goat skin thing with the spout. You do remember pouring it all over yourself don't you?"

"No. Just drive, lets get going or we won't have enough time to do what we came here to do," Russ said angrily.

Stuart smiled to himself as the car picked up speed going down the hill. They could see the road in the distance. It crossed the small valley then it climbed quite steeply up Mt Etna finally disappearing around the other side.

The road got worse the further that they went. They had now rounded the mountain so that now they could see the sea. The road had climbed very steeply and now they were only a couple of hour's hike from the top. The Mercedes rounded a bend and Stuart had to brake sharply because there in front of them was the large larva flow that Elondro had told them about.

The road at this point was a little wider as people had parked here. Most likely it was young lovers, as this was a very beautiful spot, overlooking

The land of no horizons

the water many hundreds of feet below.

Stuart turned the engine off as Russ was getting out of the car.

"Pop the trunk Stuart, I can't wait to get climbing. This doesn't look too difficult to me. What do you think?"

"No, it looks pretty easy to me. Perhaps it will get harder as we get up a bit further."

When Stuart got round to the back of the car Russell had already got out both backpacks, their hiking boots and had closed the trunk.

"You didn't need anything out of there, except your pack and boots did you," Russ asked.

"No, everything's in there, we do need that bread and meat we got in town, it's on the back seat. If you get it, I'll carry it," Stuart said, as he flung his backpack on. Russ retrieved the bag of food. He walked over to Stuart opened his pack and stuffed the food in.

At that moment Etna rumbled loudly and spit out a large cloud of steam and dust. The boys looked at each other as the ground shook but it didn't bother them too much. Living in California,

The land of no horizons

you got used to the ground shaking occasionally.

"Lets go this way," Russ said as he took the lead and started up the lava flow.

It wasn't a hard climb, not like the one in the rocky's. It was more like a hard hike. They could walk most of the time and only occasionally did they have to do any real climbing. All the time Etna was blowing out steam and the smell of sulpha was very strong. The blasts of steam and the ground shaking went hand in hand. Usually about twenty seconds after a steam blast the ground would rumble. Sometimes the rumblings were very intense. One almost knocked the boys to the ground.

The mountain had been quiet for almost half an hour and the brothers had been making good time as they headed for the top of the mountain. Out of nowhere a great blast of steam came from the volcano followed by the largest quake they had felt so far. This shock was hard enough to make the boys grab hold of large rocks, so as not to fall to the ground. From above them, small to medium size rocks rolled down the mountain side.

"That was a big one," Stuart said, " I hope we

The land of no horizons

don't get too many more of those"

"Look up there," Russ said. Pointing up the mountain side.

Stuart eyes followed Russell's finger and immediately saw what Russ was pointing at. About fifty yards ahead was a large outcrop of rocks, most were small but mixed in were some very large ones. The whole thing looked very unstable. This is where all the rocks that had just rolled past them had come from.

"They don't look very stable do they," Russ said, "another shaker like the last one and they could come down on us. I think we should get out of their pathway, just incase *they* do decide to come down."

"There's a hint of a path over to your left, let's get the hell out of here while we still have chance."

Before either of them could move, a tremendous blast of steam blew out of the volcano. The shock that followed was even larger than the last one. The ground shook for thirty seconds or more.

A few seconds later another blast, even larger than the last one. The ground shook so bad that they

The land of no horizons

both were thrown to the ground. Russ looked up towards the rocks above them and his worst fears were realized. It seemed like the whole hillside was starting to move towards them.

"*Run Stuart run*" he called out. As he turned to run downhill.

Stuart was just getting to his feet as Russ caught up to him.

"Run like your life depends on it because it probably does," Russ said. Stuart looked up the hill just in time to see the whole side of the mountain slip away and start towards them.

Russ was now a few yards ahead as Stuart scrambled to his feet and started to run. The mountain blasted out an even larger blast of dust, steam and rocks and at the same time the ground shook again. The shaking was so violent, that the ground they were standing on developed a huge crack just in front of them. As they turned to try and get around it, a second crack appeared beside them.

Without warning the ground they were standing on dropped into a black hole. Both boys hit the side of the hole as they fell fifteen feet or more.

The land of no horizons

Then they rolled at least another twenty feet before they stopped, hard against a large rock.

The whole mountain seemed to be shaking, and the noise was loud and getting louder. They both looked towards where they had fallen in, just as thousands of rocks started to fall through the hole.

It seemed like half the mountain was trying to get through the hole. "Let's get running before we get crushed," Russell said.

They both scrambled to their feet and started to run away from the hole. They were in a large cave, that didn't seem to have an end. The darkness was creeping in on them as the hole was fast disappearing behind them. A large rock as big as a car were rolling down the cave after them. Running as fast as they could, they managed to stay just ahead of the boulders. Now there was no light at all, it was pitch black, the hole that they had fallen into was gone, it was completely filled with rocks and dirt and soil.

Russ was in the lead still running as fast as he could his arms were in front of his face, to try and protect it from any rocks that might be hanging

The land of no horizons

down. Behind him, he could hear Stuart's footsteps, half a stride away. But behind that he could hear what sounded like that huge rock was still rumbling after them and getting closer by the second.

In total darkness it was scary to run as fast as they were. But with what was behind them, they had no choice. Russell couldn't see the rock coming up from the cave floor. He hit it hard with his shin and fell over it, with Stuart hitting it also and falling on top of him. Both men lay silent as the rock caught up to them. It hit the rock hard and kept on going. Stuart felt it whiz past his ear as he flattened himself against his brother, then he heard it land a short distance away and keep on rolling.

Stuart rolled of Russ's back and took in three deep breaths. "Are you ok?" He asked.

Russell was winded and his leg hurt like hell. "I think I'm ok" Russ replied, "but my leg hurts, I hope it's not broken."

As they both lay there it started to sink in the terrible situation they were in.

"Do you still have your backpack?" Stuart asked.

The land of no horizons

"Yeah" Russ said, as he sat up and slipped the bag of his back.

Stuart already had his open and was feeling his way through it, looking for one particular item. His fingers hit the metal and glass part, and he pulled it from the bottom of his bag. *I hope it's not broken* he thought as he pulled it clear. He instantly found the switch and turned it on. A beam of bright light streamed from it.

"Shine it this way," Russell said.

Stuart pointed it towards his brother and he didn't like what he saw. Russ was bleeding from his leg below the knee and he also had a cut on his forehead that was dripping blood all down his face.

"Are you sure you're ok, you look like you've been through a war or something?" Stuart said.

"I feel like I was in a war and I think I lost but under the circumstances, I'm ok."

Russ found his headlight and turned it on, he adjusted the headband and put it on his head so it sat comfortably against his forehead.

"Now that we can see, let's go see if there's a chance we can get out of here," Russ said.

The land of no horizons

Looking back, there was a large dust cloud that was slowly making its way towards them. The cloud was so dense that their lights couldn't penetrate it.

"We should take care of your leg before we do anything else, it needs cleaning and covering with something," Stuart replied.

"I'm ok," Russ said as he tried to stand. But as soon as he put some weight on his leg it gave way and he fell back down again.

"Ooo that hurts," he said, "I think I need a minute before I can go anywhere."

Stuart got a piece of paper napkin, from the food that they bought in town, poured some water on it from a bottle he had in his backpack and gave it to Russell. "Here, use this, it might help a little."

Russell took the damp napkin and placed it gently against the cut on his leg.

Stuart was looking around. The cave they where in was quite large, the roof was in most places at least fifteen feet high. Back where they had come from looked hopeless at first glance. The dust was settling now and there was absolutely no way they

The land of no horizons

could dig through that and get out. In front of them it was impossible to tell if there was an exit somewhere, or even how big the cave was. The light from Stuart's headlight didn't reach the end, the cave just seemed to go on forever.

"Well little brother, what do you think," Russ said.

"It doesn't look good. The hole we just fell through is gone, it's totally filled in with rocks and debris, it seem's to have come this way a hundred feet or more. So there's absolutely no way out that way. Our only choice, seems to be to see where this cave leads to and hope it comes out somewhere. Because if it doesn't, we could be entombed here for the rest of our lives and that won't be very long."

"Thanks for being so positive. But we do have a chance I still have my cell phone," Russ said as he pulled out his phone.

"Try it," Stuart said, "I doubt you will get a signal but its worth a try."

Russ flipped open the phone and punched in some numbers. He looked at the display screen and read *no signal*. "Piece of crap phone," he said, as he

The land of no horizons

threw it against the cave wall smashing it into tiny pieces.

"You shouldn't have done that, we might have needed that sometime," Stuart said angrily.

"Your right, sorry, I let my temper get the better of me. You still have your phone, don't you?"

"I do, if it's not broken" Stuart said as he detached his from his waistband. He flipped it open and the light came on. "Ok, so mine works. Now maybe we should take stock of what we have before we move on."

As they started to open the backpacks the ground shook again and a big rock fell from the roof of the cave missing them by only a few feet.

"Let's leave the bag check till later, I think we should move away from here while we still can," Russ said.

"Can you walk ok, your leg looks pretty bad?" Stuart asked.

"Help me up and I'll see how bad it is."

Stuart got to his feet and walked over to Russell. He held out his hand and his brother took a tight grip. Stuart pulled gently and Russ grimaced as

The land of no horizons

he slowly got to his feet. Balancing mainly on one foot and using the other just for balance, he stood there swaying, only just staying balanced.

"That hurts like hell, I could use something to lean on."

"I'll go and see if I can find you something to use as a walking stick," Stuart said as he started back the way they had come in.

Russ balanced the best that he could on one foot but he knew that he wouldn't be able to walk far without help and lots of it.

Stuart came back with a piece of tree branch about five feet long. It was not straight, or very strong but it would do in a pinch. Stuart pulled out his Swiss army knife and cut off a few little branches, before he handed it over to Russ.

Russ took it in both hands and said, "I think this will help."

Another rumble shook some more dust from above.

"Let's get moving, why we still can," Stuart said, as he scooped up both backpacks.

"How did it look back there, any chance at all

The land of no horizons

that we can come back and dig our way out?"

Stuart looked Russ in the eye, shook his head slowly, and started off down the cave.

The land of no horizons

CHAPTER FIVE

A white police car pulls slowly away from a mansion in the rich part of Sacramento. Inside the car are two senior police officers, Nancy Sorenson and deputy police chief Gordon Williams. It was a difficult job they had, and sometimes it was heart breaking even for them. Telling parents that their son's were missing and assumed dead was one of those jobs. The Barron family are very well known around California, that is why two high-ranking officers were dispatched to tell them the bad news.

"That went well, I thought," Gordon said.

"I don't know. If you ask me, they were far too calm. If that was my boy's I wouldn't react like they did. They showed almost no emotion at all.

The land of no horizons

Strange if you ask me."

"We did our job and that's all I care about. People take bad news differently. But, you are right, they did seem a bit cold, you expect a few tears when you are told your kids are dead."

Inside the house Mrs. Barron is on the couch in her fancy livingroom, tears are rolling down her face. The shock of what she has just been told is slowly sinking in. Her boys are missing, not dead, but missing. There's a big difference. She was very surprised when the police showed up at her door, she knew that both her sons liked to take risks. They loved to play hard and she was always afraid that something like this might happen but she always felt that if something did happen, she would know. She had always been close to her boys growing up. She had been like father and mother to them. Their father was busy building an empire, much too busy to be a dad. So she did everything with them. She always believed that there was some kind of telekinetic connection between them. It was something she had never told anyone, not even her

The land of no horizons

husband. But she believed it was there. Now something had happened to them and she sensed nothing.

When the boys were young she was sure that they influenced some of the decision's she made. There was one Christmas when they both got exactly the bicycle that they wanted, without showing them to her. There were lots of other times too, when there was a certain movie they wanted to see, or a restaurant they wanted to go too. They didn't ask, they didn't have to, she knew, she always knew. But now nothing.

Upstairs Lawrence was in his bathroom, sat on the floor sobbing like he had never sobbed before. His boys were *gone*. This was the most devastating news. Ever. How could this have happened? He should have insisted, that they don't take risks the way they did. All the rock climbing and the other crazy stuff that they did. Now look what's happened.

He had big plans for his son's, he wanted them to take over the business. He hoped that they could take it to the next level. He had not been a

The land of no horizons

good father, he was building their future. Now there was no future, only a past, and not a very memorable one at that.

Using his shirt sleeve he wiped the tears from his eyes. He got to his feet and went into the bedroom. On his side of the king size bed was a phone. He Picked up the phone he cradled it in his hand, then he punched in a set of numbers and waited for an answer. There was a click on the line and then a friendly male voice said "hello."

"This is Lawrence Barron, I want the plane ready to leave as soon as possible, we are going to Sicily."

"Yes Mister Barron and will there be stops along the way."

"No stops. How fast can you have it ready?"

"About an hour, sir."

"Good get it done. There will be just me and my wife."

"Very well sir, we will be ready. Is there anything else you need?"

"No."

"Then we will see you in about an hour."

The land of no horizons

When the Barron's deplaned in Palermo the chief of police for all of Sicily was waiting to greet them. He was a tall man with grey hair, he spoke with hardly a trace of an accent. He immediately gave his condolences to the Barron's and he informed them that the search for the boys had been called off, as there was nothing else that they could do. Lawrence almost jumped down his throat. "I will tell you when the search is over," he said. "And that will be when we have turned over every rock on that mountain, or we have found the boys and not before."

"Sir," the policeman said, "I understand that you are upset but we have done an extensive search of the mountain. We have had three search parties out for two days. We have had a helicopter out for over ten hours. This is not a mountain that has a lot of places to hide, and the ones that there are we know about and we searched them thoroughly. I'm very sorry but your son's are not on that mountain."

Veronica jumped in and said, "did you find any trace of the boys."

The land of no horizons

"We found the car that they were driving, where we expected to find it. But that was all."

"What do you mean where you expected to find it?" Lawrence asked.

"When your boys were driving down here, they picked up two girls who were hitch hiking. One of the girls lives here on the island, the other is a friend of hers from collage. Your boys drove them to the girls house and they stayed there for a small party for Copena. While they were there, they talked about going up the mountain and were shown a back way up Etna and told where to park. That is where we found the car. They were warned that the mountain was very unstable and that they should wait until it calmed down a bit. But sadly they chose to go on the mountain anyway."

"I see," Lawrence said. "Now this is what I need. I need a helicopter, I need at least three experienced search teams and someone to co-ordinate this. Will you help me set this up."

"But sir......

"I know that you have done the best job that you can," Lawrence said interrupting, "But I'm not

The land of no horizons

leaving this island until I have done everything in my power to find my boys. Is that clear?"

"Yes sir, that is clear."

"Oh, and don't worry I will pay for everything."

Four days have passed since the ill-fated climb of Mt Etna. The cave seems endless. It widens, it narrows, twice it has almost closed up but it left them just enough room to get though. It was as if it was leading them somewhere. There had been caves running off the main cavern, but they had all led nowhere.

Russell didn't need the long stick anymore. He could walk ok without it, he just kept it to help him, if he needed it. The boys had now gone very conservative with everything they had. They ate as little food as they could, they only used one headlight at a time. Water hadn't been a big problem until lately, as they walked along they would find water, running down the walls. They always took time to drink and fill their bottles, they knew that dehydration could be a big problem. The big worry

The land of no horizons

was that lately the water had been salty and undrinkable.

Stuart was in the lead with his light on, he looked tired and dirty, but he still had steely determination in his eyes, he was not ready to give up, not yet anyway. Russ was behind carrying his own pack and using the stick occasionally. His leg looked bruised and sore, but it was not infected and it was improving slowly. "Do you think we should take a break for a few minutes?" Russ asked.

"We can do," Stuart replied as he slumped to the cave floor and slipped his backpack off.

"It's good to get those things off," Russell said.

"You're not kidding. What direction do you think we are heading, Russ?"

"According to my compass we are heading south most of the time and south west the rest of the time."

There was a moment of quiet then Russ said, "we've been going slightly downhill almost all the time. We must be pretty deep by now. Yet the air quality is good, better than you would expect."

The land of no horizons

"I've been thinking the same thing, you would expect the air to be stale but it's not. I keep expecting to find a huge hole in the roof letting in lots of fresh air but if there is one we've not seen it. I think we must be a couple of miles down and it seems to continue the same way. I just hope that there's still air to breath when we finally get to the end of this cave." Stuart said as he turned his head looking deep into the cave.

Russell turned his light on and reached into his bag and pulled out a bottle of water, he took a small drink, swished it around his mouth, then he swallowed it. "How are you for food and water?"

"Water I have almost two bottles, food I have perhaps enough for two more day's that's all."

"I'm about the same. How about batteries for the headlights?"

"I have one spare set but that's all."

"I've got the same we need to use them sparingly if we run out of power we are as good as dead. What do you think of our chances of getting out of here?"

Stuart looked his brother in the eye and they

The land of no horizons

both said in unison, "slim to nil."

The silence in the cave was almost scary, the only sound was an occasional dripping sound, somewhere in the distance.

"We should get going again. We are doing no good sitting here felling sorry for ourselves," Stuart said.

"Yeah, your right, let me lead for a while," Russ said as he struggled to his feet.

The land of no horizons

CHAPTER SIX

Three days later, things were not getting any better. The boys were totally out of food now and only had a little water left. Russell was leading as they continued through this massive cavern system. Lately there had been many side caverns going off the main cave. The boys were too tired to go down everyone. They checked out each one as they came upon them. Some they discounted right away, some they explored a bit but they always ended up in the same main cave. On one of these side trips they made a grizzly discovery, they found a skeleton, sat down leaning against the cave wall. A sad reminder of what lay in front of them unless they get lucky.

The land of no horizons

The boys took a woman's watch off the wrist of the corps, in the hope that they could, *if they got out,* find the family of the owner and tell them what they found and where.

Finding a skeleton is not something that gives you encouragement, when you are in the situation that the brothers now found themselves in.

As the tenth day came around the boys were on their last leg's, they had not eaten anything for three days and they had only managed to lap a little water from the cave wall's. The end was not far away for both boys and they knew it.

The cave ahead narrowed greatly, as it had done many times before. The light from Russell's light hardly penetrated the darkness anymore, the batteries were getting so low in power. These were the last of the batteries, all they had left after these went, were four candles that lasted about an hour each.

Russ climbed through a narrow part of the cave and he fell on the other side. "Are you ok?" Stuart asked sounding very concerned.

The land of no horizons

"Yeah, I'm all right."

Good, then shine the light this way, so I can see where I'm going."

Russell's head popped up and Stuart climbed through the same hole.

As they sat there quietly, a huge depression seemed to come over both boys. "It's hopeless isn't it." Stuart said.

"We're not dead yet little brother, there's always a chance."

"I bet mom and dad are upset. I wish, I could contact them. Even if it's just to say goodbye."

"I know how you feel. But there's nothing we can do."

There was silence for a long moment.

"Can you hear water running?" Russell asked.

Stuart didn't answer right away, then he said "yes I think I can."

Russell got to his feet first and held down his hand to help up his brother. "Lets go before these batteries run out and we have no light at all."

The two brothers continued cautiously, down towards where they thought the water sound was

The land of no horizons

coming from. As they got closer there was defiantly water ahead somewhere.

Rounding a small bend there it was. The boys had to look twice, to see if what they thought they saw was real. There was a large rock structure, that looked like a huge saucer sat on the cave floor. It was full to the brim with water.

Russ got there first, dropping his backpack on the floor. He cupped his right hand and scooped up some water. Before he could get the water to his mouth, something, silver and red flashed out of the water towards his hand, missing only by an inch or so. "What the hell was that?" he said, as he stepped back quickly, and fell onto the cave floor.

"What was what?" Stuart asked.

"Something jumped out of the water and tried to bite me."

"Go away your nuts. ....Are you sure?"

"Of course I'm sure," Russ said as he stood up and leaned over the water. "Something leapt out of the water and tried to bite my finger's off."

Both brother's leaned over and looked closely into the dark water. Sure enough, just an inch or so

The land of no horizons

below the water level, swam hundred's of tiny fish. Darting about at a speed faster than any fish, they had ever seen. It was as if they stopped they would be dead.

Stuart laughed, "are you scared of those little things?"

"That's not what jumped out of the water at me. Stand back and I'll show you."

Russell took off his backpack and dangled the end of one of his straps into the water. Two seconds later he whipped it out as fast as he could. Two fish where attached to the strap as it left the water. One fish fell back into the water, the other fell on the cave floor and flipped around like crazy.

Stuart turned his light on so he could get a better look at the fish. "Wow, look, it has no eyes, it's completely blind. And look at its teeth, it has teeth like a Piranha. What the hell kind of fish is this, I have never seen anything like it, it's weird."

The fish was about seven inches long, with a silver body and a hint of red in the tail. The body was flat and was about five inches tall at its highest point.

The land of no horizons

Stuart was into fish and animal's. He spent one summer volunteering at the San Diego Zoo. He also worked part time in a few pet shops. If Stuart could he would like to be a Vet, looking after exotic animals at a small zoo somewhere. That was his ultimate dream as a kid and still was.

"What do you think it is?" Russell asked.

"*I have no idea,* I think this is a fish that has never been seen in the outside world. There are blind cave fish that come from Africa, they are totally blind like this one but they don't look anything like this. This looks like it is part of the Barb family but with teeth. Big teeth.

"Can you eat these Barb fish?" Russell asked.

"I would think so, some grow over two feet in length, I'm sure you could eat those. But this one is not very big is it."

"We eat Sardines don't we and they are a lot smaller than this one. And there seems to be a few in there and they are not hard to catch."

"How would we cook them?"

"We could boil them. We have candles and I still have that soup can, from the first day we were

The land of no horizons

down here. Lets give it a try, we have nothing to lose."

Russell got the soup can filled it with water and then using some rocks, he made a small platform to place the can on. Placing the lite candle underneath, the water soon started to boil.

Russ had cut the head and tail off the fish. Then he cut it into two fillets, at the same time scraping out the bits, that he didn't think they should eat. Then he popped it into the boiling water.

Twenty minutes later he pulled one piece out and passed it over to Stuart. The second one he kept for himself. Nervous eyes flashed between each other, then Russell placed a piece in his mouth. He closed his eyes as he moved it around his mouth, then he chewed it and swallowed. "It's not the best fish that I've eaten, but under the circumstances it's not that bad," he said as he ate another piece.

Stuart took a small piece and popped it into his mouth. He chewed if for a short time, then he swallowed it. "Your right it's not good but it's better than starving."

*   *   *

The land of no horizons

The light from the candle flickered strange shapes on the cave walls, as both boys sat leaned up against the cave wall. "I think I'm going to be sick," Stuart said.

"Me to," Russell replied. "I think it's because we've not eaten for a couple of days that we feel this way."

"You're probably right. I think we should blow out the candle and see if we can get some sleep before we move on."

Stuart was closer to the candle, so he crawled over, blew it out, and scrambled back to where he was sitting. The total darkness was very oppressive. It seemed to close in on them, smothering them.

"How do you think those fish survive down here, there's no food for them?" Russell asked.

"I think that the big fish eat the smaller fish, and the smaller fish eat the smallest fish. And the baby fish eat tiny particles that are in the water."

"Is it possible to survive down here like that?"

"Yes, it probably is. There are some lakes in Africa, that have very little natural food in them, but they have lots of fish. The way they survive is to

The land of no horizons

have large broods of babies. Every species in the lake have lots and lots of babies. They estimate that out of every ten thousand babies born, only one grows up to be an adult. All the rest get eaten. I think we have something similar here."

"I'm glad I'm not a fish," Russell said.

"Me too."

The land of no horizons

CHAPTER SEVEN

With total darkness all around them, sleep just seemed like a natural thing to do. It was just as Stuart was dropping off to sleep that he thought he heard something. "Russ did you hear that?"

"Hear what? No, I didn't hear anything. You were dreaming."

"Shush, I did hear something," Stuart said, his voice a little more than a whisper.

"Are you sure? What did it sound like?

"I'm not positive, but I think it was a bird."

"A bird, what kind of bird?"

"Shush, just be quiet for a minute and let's listen."

The silence was overwhelming, the only

The land of no horizons

sound was that of the water running out of the pond, and disappearing somewhere down a hole, away from where they were.

Five minutes passed. Then ten. Nothing, absolutely nothing. Neither of them heard anything. "Sorry Stuart but you must have been dreaming."

"I wasn't, I heard something, I know I did." Stuart said in a desperate voice. "I know it sounds weird, hearing a bird down here, but I'm positive I heard something and I think it was a bird."

"Do you know what kind of bird?"

"No, it was very faint and only for a second that....... there it is again. Did you hear it that time?"

"I heard it, I heard it," Russell said excitedly. "But where did it come from?"

Stuart turned his light on and looked over at his brother, "I couldn't tell, could you?"

"No it was too faint. We should take up positions at either end of this chamber and hope we can get a direction."

"Good idea," Stuart said, as he scrambled to his feet. "I'll take this side, you go over there somewhere and lets hope we hear it again."

The land of no horizons

Russell headed over towards the far side of the cave. It was only then that he realized that they were at a junction in the cave, with large passages running off both ways.

With only a little light coming from the head light's the cave looked very daunting and a little scary. Without light their days were surely numbered.

The minutes passed like hours, both brothers straining to hear that elusive sound whatever it was. It was Stuart that yelled out "did you hear that?"

"No, nothing, did you hear it?"

"Yes, come over here."

Russell ran over to where Stuart was standing. "You heard it again, are you sure?"

"Yes, I think it's a Macaw"

"A *Macaw,* go away, how can it be a Macaw, they come from South America even I know that."

"Your right they do."

"Well we are thousands of miles away from there. So explain to me how can it possibly be a Macaw?"

"I don't know, but it sounds like a Macaw. If

The land of no horizons

it's not then it's a parrot of some kind. But I don't think the sound came from down this passage on my side of the cave."

Russell was stunned. "Not from down there, it didn't come from my side either," he said pointing down his side of the cave. "Then where did it come from?"

"I'm not sure, lets be quiet and if we hear it again hopefully we can tell."

Again the boys sat quietly, their breathing quiet and shallow, ears straining but all they heard was the tiny drip, drip, drip, of water coming out of the pool.

After half an hour or more, Russell got up and went to the pond, cupping up a quick handful of water, he took a small drink. At that second they both heard the loudest squawk they had heard. "Did you hear that one."

I did, but I'm still not sure where it's coming from."

"I know. It came from down that hole," Russell said, pointing at the hole, where the water

The land of no horizons

from the pond disappeared from sight.

"Are you sure?" Stuart asked.

"*Oh yeah,* I'm sure."

They both crouched down to look into the hole. With both lights shining down the hole they couldn't see much. The hole was just about big enough for them to fit into. The problem was they could only see about six feet, then it turned down and disappeared out of sight. What lay around that bend was anybody's guess. It could drop down for hundreds of feet, or it could close up so that they can't get through.

"What do you think?" Stuart asked.

"I don't know. We can't see very far. But I think we have go for it. To stay here is certain death, if we go down there we have a chance, a slight chance, but a chance."

"Ok Russ, I'm with you, do you want me to go first or do you want to do it?"

"I'll go" Russ said

The land of no horizons

CHAPTER EIGHT

It was with great trepidation that Russell slid into the small black hole. The entrance to the hole was only just big enough for him to squeeze through. Once inside he pulled his backpack through.

The water was cold as he moved slowly down the passageway. He was lying on his back and going feet first. That trickle of cold water going down his back was very uncomfortable. The bottom of the cave was very smooth, as if water had run here for hundreds of years.

Russell's light had very little power left and

The land of no horizons

Stuart's had even less. It would be a miracle if Stuart's batteries lasted more than half an hour longer and progress down this hole was very slow. When their lights finally give out, they would have no back up. The candles would not work at all in these very damp conditions. The little trickle of water had slowly increased, so that now it was a small stream that covered their whole bodies with cold, cold water. It was hard work riddling through this small hole and trying to keep their faces up out of the water.

"Are you ok?" Russell asked.

"Yeah, I'm ok but I'm worried about my light. There's not much power left in these batteries. Can you go any faster?"

"No, not really...... Can you hear that? It sounds like water rushing. We could be in big trouble if it is."

As they edged their way slowly along, they could hear the rushing water sound, getting louder and louder. The cave widened slightly, just before they reached the second stream.

Russell was sitting on the edge of the larger

The land of no horizons

stream, when Stuart got there. "That water looks cold," Stuart said.

Russell didn't answer, he looked upstream, then downstream, each one looking worse than the other. The stream was about five feet across. The water *did* look cold and black almost like ink. In the distance down stream, there was a lot of water noise. It was as if the water was picking up speed and going over rocks or rapids.

Both boys listened intensely, not happy about what they were hearing. It was hard to tell how deep the stream was, or how fast it was running. The only good thing was the cave was high enough, that they could stand upright while they were in the water.

"What do you think Stuart? Can we make it down there?" Russell said, as he took a long look downstream.

"I wish we had a choice but we don't. We can't go back. So we have to go on, it's the only chance we have." At that second Stuart's light dimmed dramatically. "We have to go now, or we might have to go in the dark and I don't like that idea one little bit."

The land of no horizons

"I'll go first," Russell said as he slipped his backpack on. He slid off the bank and into the stream and sank up to his chest in the cold black water.

The water pushed him faster than he wanted to go, but he had no choice, there was no turning back now.

"Are you ok?" Stuart shouted.

"I'm ok, the current is a lot stronger than I thought it would be."

Russell was now starting to disappear into the darkness of the cave as Stuart slipped on his backpack and jumped into the water.

Stuart"s feet hit the bottom of the stream and he instantly lost his footing. His whole body and his face went into the water. When he came up he was very cold but relieved to see his light still worked. Looking down stream he couldn't see Russ. He yelled out "Russ, are you there?" there was no reply.

The water noise was getting louder and the currant was also picking up speed. The cave had widened considerably now and there in the distance is what Russell didn't want to see. Large rocks in

The land of no horizons

the water narrowing the stream. Russell could no longer reach the bottom of the stream, he was being tossed around, he had absolutely no control.

Stuart was now a long way behind but starting to move faster with the current. His headlight gave out almost no light. He felt that he only had a couple of minutes left and then he would be in total darkness. The noise ahead was getting closer, he knew they were in trouble, big trouble.

Russell was being buffeted around by the fast-moving water. Many times he hit the rocks and every time he tried to grab hold but the rocks were to smooth and the water was just to fast. The darkness in the cave made it even scarier, he could only see a few feet ahead and then total blackness. He was worried about Stuart. He hoped his light was still working.

When Stuart's light finally died he wasn't surprised. Now in total darkness he was very scared. The noise coming from downstream was terrifying, he could sense what was ahead even though he couldn't see it. All he could do was to stick out his hands and feet in front of him, to try and cushion

The land of no horizons

any blows that were coming his way.

The churning waters tossed him around, like clothes in a washing machine. He couldn't see the rocks that threatened his life, he only hoped that Russ had made it through ok.

The water picked him up and threw him against rock after rock. He felt that his backpack was keeping him afloat, holding him up, saving his life. There was a sudden fast drop that took his breath away then he hit a large rock, first with his shoulder then his head. The blow almost rendered him unconscious. As he was tossed around in the current, he thought he heard a spine chilling scream. It had to be Russ.

Only just conscious, he sensed the water slowing. The noise was now behind him, he thought. Ahead he could hear something new. A new noise, even more frightening than before. *Waterfall*. Suddenly the stream narrowed it was now racing ahead at breakneck speed. Stuart felt like he was floating, or flying, or falling he didn't know which.

He hit the water with his back, the force of which expelled any air he had in his lungs. He

The land of no horizons

slowly sank below the water. His senses were mixed up, he was calm as he sank almost to the bottom. Then there was a feeling that someone was trying to grab him, clawing at his clothes. Pulling him. Forcing him out of the water. Dragging him onto a beach or dry land. Face down he coughed and choked, spitting up water, trying to breath, trying to make sense of what was going on.

"Stuart, are you all right?" Russell asked.

Hands were grabbing at him, trying to turn him over.

Things were blurry as Stuart tried to clear his eyes. It was light. There were three shapes hovering over him. *Have I died*, he wondered? His eyes slowly focused. *I have died,* there's an angel looking down on me. And next to her is an older man with grey hair and beard. He was dressed in a shirt that was full of holes, and his shorts were just as bad. Is that god? Standing next to him is Russ.

"Russ, did you die too?"

"No, we didn't die we are alive, we made it, we are outside!"

"Well, sorry old boy, but I hate to brake this to

The land of no horizons

you but you are not *out,* if by *out* you mean, you are back on the surface of this planet earth," the old man said, in a very English accent.

"What do you mean?" Russell said as he looked around, totally confused by what he saw.

Stuart could not take his eyes of the angel looking down at him. She had the most wonderful eyes that he had ever seen. They were blue, like a pure blue crystal. The face, that they were set in was so beautiful she had to be an angel. Her smile was out of this world and surrounding her face was long golden blonde hair.

"Are you ok?" she asked, also in an English accent.

Is god and all the Angels English? Stuart thought.

"Yes, I think I'm ok," Stuart stammered, as he sat up. It was only then that he noticed his angel, was wearing something that looked like a bikini. Not something that was bought in a store but something that was homemade. It was made out of animal skin. The top only just covered her breasts and the bottom was just a matching piece of skin,

The land of no horizons

that came up between her legs and was flipped over a string tied around her waist.

Stuart slipped of his backpack, as he was still trying to make sense of what was going on. He wasn't in heaven, that he knew. But where were they? And who were these people?

Is this a dream, or am I going nuts? Russell thought, as he spun around trying to take in what his eyes were seeing. They were out in the light, on the bank of a stream surrounded by trees and lush plants. But when he looked up there was no sun, no sky. There was a *roof,* a cave roof, a very high cave roof, but a roof just the same. "I don't understand, where the hell are we?" He asked.

"I wish I could tell you that young man but sorry to say I can't." the man said. "I can introduce myself. My name is Professor Lionel Summers and this is my daughter Carrie."

"Hi, my name is Russell, and this is my brother Stuart."

"Ah, you are Americans," Lionel said.

"It's nice to meet you," Carrie said. "It's lucky for you that we were fishing, or you might have

The land of no horizons

drowned. Stuart are you sure you are ok, you look a little weird."

Stuart was having difficulty believing what was happening around him. They were not outside but they could see, there was light. There was also the most beautiful girl that he had ever seen leaning over him. Talking to him in an English accent. It made no sense, no sense at all.

Stuart shook his head, blinked a couple of times and she was still there.

"Do you need help getting up?" She said, as she held down her hand, to help him up.

"No, I think I'm ok," Stuart said.

Russell looked at Stuart, he looked all right, a bit dazed, a few scratches, but ok. He took stock of himself, a few bumps and bruises but when he thought of what they had just been through they looked great. Taking a closer look at Stuart he did look a little strange, he couldn't take his eyes off Carrie. Then as he took a closer look at Carrie he could see why.

Carrie came over to where Russell and Lionel where standing and said, "daddy, we should take

The land of no horizons

them back to our camp, so that they can rest. And they might be hungry?"

"You are right my dear, what am I thinking. Come along boys, it's only a short distance to our camp."

Carrie seemed to want to lead the way as she started to walk towards a small gap in the foliage. Her father was just a few steps behind her.

Russell leaned over to Stuart and said, "do these two seem a bit strange to you?"

"No, they're just British. The brit's can be a little eccentric, you know that. We've met a few weird ones on our travels, right?"

"Yeah, we have met a few eccentric British people, but these two seem very strange to me."

"Never mind that now, just pick up your bag and lets follow them, they say they have food."

"Ok, but keep a close eye on them until we get to know them better."

Stuart picked up his backpack and said, "oh, I intend to keep a close eye on them, a very close eye."

"I don't mean just on the girl, I mean on both

The land of no horizons

of them."

"You can watch Lionel and I'll watch Carrie. Is that ok with you?"

"You know that's not what I meant," Russell said, sounding a little annoyed.

"I'm just pulling your leg. I know what you mean but I think that you're over reacting. I think that they are harmless and we are lucky to have found them. So pick up you bag and lets go after them before we get lost, again."

Russell picked up his bag and Stuart gave him a push in the direction that Lionel and Carrie had gone. Before leaving this little beach on the side of the stream, he took a look around.

The water was crystal clear in the lagoon, in the roof of the cave was a hole where the water poured in. *So that's how we arrived in this strange world,* he thought. Near the water spout were some vines and sat on those vines were two beautiful Blue and Gold Macaws. They were squabbling and fighting and occasionally one of them would let out a big squawk. *"Thanks guys you saved our lives,"* he said quietly.

The land of no horizons

"Come on Stuart," Russell said, from somewhere just out of sight.

"I'm coming, I'm coming," Stuart replied.

The land of no horizons

CHAPTER NINE

The path was very winding and narrow, the bush around them was dense like you might expect in the amazon, or the thick jungles of Africa. So they walked in a single file, with Stuart being last and unable to see Carrie, who was still leading the way.

The tree's were huge reaching a hundred feet or more. And between the trees was thick undergrowth, shrubs, bushes, so thick you could only see a few feet. Yet it was alive, there were all kinds of noises. Some were loud, like monkeys screeching in the tree tops. Some were subtle, like insects whispering, calling each other, somewhere, not too far away.

The land of no horizons

As they walked Stuart noticed that the trees seemed to be thinning out a little, when all of a sudden they were out of the jungle and into a large clearing. Russell had caught up to the professor and was walking by his side. Stuart sped up his steps and caught up also.

Carrie was still a few yards ahead when Stuart finally took a position on the other side of the professor.

The clearing was huge. Almost round in shape, at least the size of five football fields. The grass was thick and lush, and over on the other side were two dozen deer grazing away calmly, as if they had not a care in the world.

Stuart was speechless as he looked around. Was it the bump on his head, or was it just too surreal to believe what his eyes were seeing? Except for the cave roof above their heads, they could be anywhere in the world that has lush rain forest.

"Professor, where exactly do you think we are?" Russell asked.

"That's a stupid question, we are under Africa of course."

The land of no horizons

"*Africa,*" the boys said, in unison.

"Of course Africa......you boys weren't in Africa when you started your journey here, were you?"

"No we were in Sicily. On Mt Etna, when we got trapped in a landslide and ended up here," Russ said.

"Sicily hmm, now that's interesting. How long ago was that?" Lionel asked.

Stuart looked at his watch and said, " that was ten days ago."

"So in ten days you walked all the way from Sicily, under the Mediterranean Sea to here. Now that is amazing. Tell me what time is it."

"It's four thirty," Stuart said.

"And what day and year is it."

"It's Wednesday the first of August two thousand and seven" Stuart said.

The professor slowed his steps, "two thousand and seven," he said.

"Yes sir," Russell said. Surprised at the professor's reaction.

"It's been almost nine years...... Nine years

The land of no horizons

we have been down here."

No one spoke for the next few minutes. Everyone seemed deep in their own thought's.

As they walked across that clearing Lionel saw Carrie in a new light. She had always been his little girl. But now as she walked in front of him, he noticed that she was not a little girl anymore. She had grown up without him seeing it. She was a young woman, there was a swish in her hips that he had never noticed. She had the curves of a young woman. But she was dressed in a way that showed off too much of her, much too much. Especially now that there were young men around. He had not noticed how his daughter had grown up, but he didn't doubt that they had noticed.

Carrie was a short distance in front, when she turned around and shouted, "we'll be there soon."

Just in front of them was what looked like a pile of rocks about three feet high. Just as Carrie got close to it, it got up and started to slowly move away. Carrie took no notice to it as she walked away past it. As Stuart and Russell got closer they could see it was a giant Tortoise, just munching on grass

The land of no horizons
and ambling along.

Stuart was amazed, he had seen a giant Tortoise's but he was sure that they didn't get that big. He opened his mouth to say something, when out of the jungle there came a deep roar. "What was that?" He asked.

"That my boy is a Saber-Toothed Tiger."

Stuart's mouth dropped open, "how can that be, they've been extinct for thousands of years. Do you really expect me to believe that, that noise came from a Saber-Toothed Tiger?"

"It's up to you. If you don't believe me, you'll see for yourself soon."

"What do you mean by that?" Russell asked.

"He usually sits on a big rock that overlooks our camp. He likes to come down and take one of our goats, now and again."

Russ and Stuart were looking at each other in total disbelief. Having crossed the clearing, they now started down another narrow path. Carrie was still leading the little group, as they walked down the narrow path between tall trees and dense undergrowth. On the breeze was the sweet smell of

The land of no horizons

flowers mixed with the scent of grass and damp forest.

The jungle started to thin out again and as they broke free of the trees, the boys again were astonished at the sight that they now looked upon.

Instead of walking on grass, they were walking on sand. In front of them was a beach. As beautiful a beach as you would see on any tropical island. And there was water lapping onto this beach. At either side of the water were cliffs going all the way up to the cave roof. In the distance, looking out over the water was what appeared to be a large island covered in tall trees.

Carrie was heading towards a cave in the rock face. There was a rough fence in front of the cave opening. Behind the fence there were about twenty goats running around. When Carrie reached the fence, she opened a makeshift gate and passed through it.

Russell and Stuart were speechless, as they followed behind the professor as he went through the gate.

"Please close the gate after you, it helps to

The land of no horizons

keep the goats in," Lionel said.

Stuart did as he was asked because he was the last one in. Inside the fenced area was quite large, about one third was sand and two thirds grass. It covered a space about half the size of a football field.

On the grass but close to the entrance of the cave, was a roughly made table and a bench at either side. As the three men got close to the table, Carrie came out of the cave carrying a big leaf full of fruits and berries.

"Sit down please," Carrie said as she placed the leaf on the table. "Now eat and we will talk later."

The brothers dropped their backpacks sat on one of the benches and started to eat. There were all kinds of fruit, bananas, pineapples, and some small white fruit about the size of a very large apple. There were also three different kinds of berries, all tasting very sweet but very different. To finish the meal, there was salted meat, that tasted like beef jerky, and coconut milk to wash it all down.

The boys ate ravenously savoring each morsel

The land of no horizons

as they ate it. It was a banquet like none they had ever tasted before. It was unique and delicious

"While you guys are eating, perhaps I should tell you how we got here," Lionel said.

"Please do professor, I can't wait to here it," Russell said.

"Well, were should I start. Carrie and I are missionaries', we have spent lots of time in all kinds of god forsaken places. But our last one was in Tunisia, which is northern Africa. We were based in a village called El Jura. It's just a small place about ten miles inland from the Mediterranean Sea."

"Besides doing our missionary work I also tried to use my skills as a doctor to help heal the sick whenever I could. One day we got a call to go and see a woman who was expecting a baby in a few weeks. She lived about two miles from where we were staying. We drove about one mile then the road stopped completely, so we started to walk. The village where the woman lived was at the base of a large hill, as we got close to the village a huge bull Elephant appeared out of the bush. The poor creature was in great pain, there was a huge hole in

The land of no horizons

his face where he had been shot."

"The animal was crazed with pain. He charged at us forcing us back along the trail. We knew this trail well, as we had traveled it a few times before. We knew that there was a cave and we got there just before the Elephant did. He was mad, he attacked the front of the cave until he caused a landslide that blocked the cave entrance. We were trapped. In my doctor's bag I had a torch, *what you Americans call a flashlight*. Well, to cut a long story short, two days later we found ourselves here. We came in close to the grand canal. And as the saying goes, we have been here ever since."

"Carrie darling, Russell tells me it is now August two thousand and six. You know what that means? We have been here for almost nine years. It also makes you, twenty-one year's old."

"I don't know what to say. Nine years is a long time," she said.

While the professor had been telling their story, Russell had been watching Stuart. He had been listening to what Lionel had been saying but he had been watching Carrie. Carrie tried not to notice

The land of no horizons

Stuart looking at her but she kept glancing his way and a little smile came to her lips when she caught him looking.

"There are just the two of you, is their professor?" Stuart asked.

"No actually there are three of us". Jo Jo is the other one. He is our guide and our friend, he likes to go off hunting on his own. Sometimes he's gone for days, then he comes back with some meat or something we can use. He's a very valuable part of our little family. Without him we would have died many years ago."

"So for us it is nice to have you here, the only thing is that for you, it may be a life sentence as I don't think there is a way out of here."

"Professor, speaking for myself and I'm sure for my brother, I'm just happy to be alive. Because if we had not found this place and you, within a few days we would be dead, of that I'm sure. So we are here and while we are here we will search every corner of this cave until we find a way out for all of us," Russell said.

"That may be a bigger challenge than you

The land of no horizons

think. But before we get into that, would you happen to have a pair of binoculars?" Lionel asked.

"Yes we do, would you like to use them?" Stuart asked.

"Oh, yes please," Lionel said excitedly.

Stuart dug around in his backpack feeling for the small binoculars that he knew were in there somewhere. Finally his fingers touched the soft plastic case and he pulled them out. He passed them over to Lionel who smiled like he had just been given the best present ever.

"Thank you, my boy. These are very nice, they look very expensive," he said, as he put them to his eyes and looked around. He seemed to be studying one rock face in particular. Finding what he wanted to see he adjusted the focus on the binoculars. Then he passed them over to Stuart. "Can you see that ledge just above the tree line?" He said pointing towards the far side of the cave.

Stuart took the glasses, put them up to his eyes and looked in the general direction that the professor had pointed. His eyes soon found the ledge and when they did he said, "oh my god, I don't believe

The land of no horizons

it!"

"What is it?" Russell asked.

"Take a look," Stuart said as he passed the binoculars over to Russ.

Russell took the glasses put them to his eyes, adjusted them slightly and scanned the far wall. He found the ledge and sat there was what looked like a Tiger. It was pale in color similar to the white tigers they had seen in Las Vegas. This one looked big, it's head was facing the other way. When it's large head swung forward Russ gave a large gasp. There sticking out of its upper jaw were two very large fangs. "If I hadn't seen it, I wouldn't have believed it, it's a Saber-Toothed Tiger," he said.

The land of no horizons

CHAPTER TEN

"Professor, it's raining. How can it rain, we are in a cave it doesn't make any sense that it can rain, but it is?" Stuart said.

"If you can wait just a little while I think I can explain exactly how things work down here," Lionel said.

The small group had left the camp and they headed down the same path as yesterday. But when they reached the large field they followed the tree line until they came upon another path. This path cut back into the forest again. Carrie was leading the way with Lionel behind her, followed by Stuart and Russ was last man in the line.

Carrie was wearing a pair of shorts and a T-

The land of no horizons

shirt she got from Stuart. Before the boys went to sleep yesterday they saw an animated argument between Lionel and Carrie. It wasn't difficult to figure out what it was about. Carrie was looking at the clothes she was wearing and saying what's wrong with them. Lionel was trying to make her see that now that there were other men around, she needed to cover herself up a bit more. It wasn't hard to guess that she didn't have anything else to wear, so Stuart stepped in and offered her some of his clothes. She reluctantly accepted, which made Lionel happy. Neither brother had any shoes that fit her but that wasn't really a problem, Carrie was used to going barefoot.

The path through the bush was well worn with one rut down the middle. In some parts the path closed right in on the group, in others it opened right up so that they could see for long distances. They crossed a large stream of crystal clear water. Then they followed the bank for a short time.

The jungle noise was unexpected, it was loud and diverse. There was a monkey somewhere screaming its head off. The bug's made so much

The land of no horizons

noise, clicking sounds, chirping sounds, whistling sounds they seemed to be all around them closing in and moving away.

Animals were everywhere Antelope with long straight horns. Deer about the size of a large dog. Birds filled the trees Toucans with their large colorful beaks, doves, and so many types of parrots that you couldn't count them.

Stuart was awed by the whole thing. It was nature as god had intended it. But where were the predators, there had to be predators to keep everything in balance. They had seen the Sabertooth tiger but there had to be more than that.

All of a sudden the landscape was changing. The ground was now rock and shale instead of soil and grass. All the trees were now behind them. The path had disappeared with the harder ground. Looking back Russell could see over the tree tops as they started to climb.

The rain had stopped now. When it was looking like there was nowhere to go, a path was cut into the rock side. Carrie was still leading the way, her bare feet on the hard rock didn't seem to bother

The land of no horizons

her. Up ahead Stuart could see were they were heading, a large flat shelf sticking out from the cliff face. From there they would be able to see everything.

Reaching the shelf only took a few minutes and as expected they could see the whole valley below. Lionel and Carrie stood back and watched the boys as they surveyed the scene before their eyes.

Stuart stepped close to the edge as he looked around. The panorama was spectacular, the trees dense in some places, yet there were clearings lots of them. And flowers all over the place, pockets of bright red, shimmering violet and subtle purple. To the right was the water, with the big island in the middle of it. He could see the beach and the small fenced area, where the goats were kept. There also was the small cave, that was to serve as their home. A short distance away there was the big field, that they had crossed earlier. Looking in front of them and to the left was jungle, thick jungle, with a hundred shades of green. The most surprising thing, was the sheer size of the place, it was massive. It

The land of no horizons

was like a huge valley you might find in any mountainous part of the world. The only difference was that instead of sky up above, there was the cave roof.

Looking down from this spot Russell realizes what a task it would be to find a way out of this place. If there is a way back up to the surface finding it will be almost impossible, he thought.

As he looked across the cave, he estimated it to be almost three and a half miles across and about twenty miles long, if not longer. And that was what he could see, there were valley's leading of the main valley that he couldn't see into. This was a very big place to search for a way out.

"You shouldn't stand so close to the edge," Lionel said, "the fumes from below can make you dizzy."

"Fumes, what fumes," Stuart said, as he looked down. He immediately stepped back when he saw what was below him.

"We call that the Grand Canal," Carrie said.

Russell stepped forward and looked down. "Is that a stream of molten larva, down there?" He

The land of no horizons

asked.

"Oh, it's far more than a stream, it's more like a river and it is very important to the whole eco system down here. The Grand Canal is the equivalent to the sun on the surface," Lionel said.

"Ok professor, explain, please," Stuart said.

"Well now where should I start. I know. Look over to your right. You can see the water, well that's salt water! Yes it is a *sea*. There are fish in there just like you would find in the Red Sea or the Mediterranean Sea. I think that I have seen sharks in there too, so be careful if you go swimming."

Now look at the dome over the sea. You can see that it is a real dome. What happens is that water evaporates off the sea and collects in the dome. You can see now that there are just a few wisps of cloud or mist in there. That's because it has just rained. Over the next few days you will see that mist thicken up. When the dome fills completely it starts to spill out into the main cave. And when that happens it seems to cause a vacuum that sucks out all the mist. Now if you look at the roof of the main cave, you will notice that it is twice as high as the

The land of no horizons

roof over the sea." Lionel stopped for a second seaming to collect his thoughts, then he said. "So all the mist rises up to the top of the main cave and cool's, causing the mist to turn back into water, rain. What you saw today was a typical rain storm down here, it rains lightly for twenty minutes to half an hour then it stops."

Lionel cautiously stepped forward and looked over the edge, "That's about the average height of the Grand Canal but it varies a lot and when it is high the temperature in the cave goes up. That causes more evaporation, which collects in the roof of the main cave. Then when the moisture from over the sea spills out, we get a severe storm, that can last for many hours. These storms are so bad we stay in the cave whenever they happen."

"Professor, I don't understand where the light comes from," Russell said.

Lionel held up his hand and said, "I was just getting to that. I told you that the Grand Canal was like the sun, but it doesn't give off enough light to illuminate this big valley. This is where this place is unique in the whole world. There is a moss that lives

The land of no horizons

in the cracks and crevices of this cave and it has the ability to collect light. Then it increases the intensity of the light and sends it back out again." Lionel walked over to the cave wall and pulled a small piece of green vegetation from the cave wall. He studied it closely then he passed it to Stuart. "Look closely at this piece of moss and you will see what I mean."

Stuart turned it over in his hand and to him it looked like an ordinary piece of moss. Then he noticed tiny specks of light emanating from some of the fronds of the moss. "I see some tiny specs of light, do you mean that they are what lights this whole cavern?"

"Precisely, my boy. That's exactly what I mean. Those tiny specs of light multiplied by millions more and you have enough light to preserve life as you see it," the professor held out his arms like an orchestra conductor who had just finished a great recital.

"That is amazing," Russell said as he looked closely at the piece of moss. "How do you think all this came about?"

The land of no horizons

"That, I'm afraid I cannot tell you. The one thing that I know for a fact, is that it has been going on for thousands of years."

"How can you be sure of that?" Russell asked.

"Well, you have seen the proof yourselves. You have seen a Saber-Toothed Tiger and they have been extinct on the surface for about ten thousands years, correct?"

"That's true. Are there other animals down here, that are extinct on the surface, are there any *dinosaurs?*" Stuart asked.

"We haven't seen any dinosaurs but we have heard strange noises coming from the island."

Stuart said, "do you think that they could be dinosaur noises?"

"I certainly wouldn't rule it out," Lionel said.

Russell had been studying the terrain when he spotted something interesting. "Professor, is that smoke coming from that clearing over there."

Lionel turned and looked, "yes it is. Do you have your binoculars with you?"

"I have," Russell said as he took the binoculars from the case and he passed them over to

The land of no horizons

Lionel.

"I like these binoculars, mine I dropped into the Grand Canal a few years ago now and I miss them." Lionel put the strap around his neck so that he couldn't lose them. Then he brought them up to his eyes and looked at the smoke for a second or two.

"Remember I told you that we were not the only people down here. Well, that smoke is from one of the two tribes of natives living down here. That is the North camp as we call it."

"Natives, you never said anything about natives." Stuart said.

"I know, I missed that bit out didn't I."

"You certainly did," Russell said.

"Come on dad tell them about natives, or do you want me too?"

"No my dear, I'll tell them, just give me a chance."

"As I said there are two tribes living with us down here. Where the smoke is coming from is the predominantly male tribe. There are about forty of them. Mostly men, a few women, and some boys.

The land of no horizons

There is only one baby girl, that lives there."

"That's strange, isn't it Professor?" Stuart asked.

"Not as strange as you think, because over there," he said, pointing to a large clearing almost on the other side of the cave, "is a tribe of women only. I should say women and their female children. That we call the South camp."

"I don't understand Professor, how can there be only women, and girl baby's?" Russell asked.

"It's very simple, but not very nice." Lionel said. " It's the women down here that rule, they are the aggressors. The men try and stay away from them. But sometimes the women need the services of a man. So what they do, is kidnap one. Then they take him back to their camp and make him do his manly duties. After about a month or so, if he's lucky, they will let him go. If he's not lucky, then they have a little ceremony and they push him into the Grand Canal."

"You mean kill him. In a sacrifice?" Stuart asked.

"I'm not sure if it's a sacrifice or punishment

The land of no horizons

for something he didn't do. I have seen it done and it is not very pretty."

"Have you tried to step in and stop it?" Russell said.

"Oh no. As I said the women are the dominant tribe down here and even if there was something I could do, I wouldn't. They have been down here living their life for thousands of years. We are only here for a short time. We have to respect their way of life and do as little as possible to impact on how they live. Also they at the moment leave us alone but if we interfered in their lives they may not like that. If we stay out of their way, we stand a better chance of survival."

"I see what you're saying, but how can you stand by and watch a man get murdered?" Stuart said.

"It's difficult but I don't carry a weapon and there are as many as twenty of them, and they are all carrying spears, what could I do?"

"I'm sorry professor. Of course you couldn't stop it. It just seems wrong to watch someone get killed, that's all," Russell said.

The land of no horizons

"I completely understand. I have only seen it twice in all the time that I have been here and believe me it is very upsetting."

"Where do they do it, daddy?"

"Can you see that big flat rock that sticks out over the canal, it's about three quarters of a mile away? Well that's the place. They get him to kneel down close to the edge. Then most of the tribe dance around him naked. Yelling and screaming. Not for long time less than ten minutes. Then the queen comes over and pushes him in." Lionel hesitated for a second or two then he said, "there is one thing that really puzzles me."

"What's that, dad?"

"When they are pushed in, they don't scream. They go silently to their deaths. Very strange."

"Ok, so they kidnap one of the men and about nine months later, babies start to appear. What do they do with the baby boys?" Russell asked.

The professor did not answer. He shuffled and tried to avoid the question.

"Dad, tell us what happens to the baby boys?"

"I prefer not to talk about it."

The land of no horizons

"Dad, I want to know. So tell us now, *please*."

"Ok, sometimes the women don't want to give up their baby's and they go and live with the men. That is why there are a few of them over there. But most of the male baby's, are left out in the jungle and the animals feed on them."

"You must be joking professor, no mother could leave her baby out to be eaten by wild animals." Stuart said. "I don't believe that."

"I'm sorry but it's true, I could hardly believe it myself. But it's true."

As Stuart turned away in disgust, he looked out towards the large clearing and as he did seven women left the trees on the far side of the clearing and started to cross the open space. "Look" he said as he pointed towards the clearing.

Four sets of eyes focused on the clearing.

"Ah, now you can see some of the women from the south village," Lionel said.

The small group of women wandered slowly across the clearing, obviously in no hurry.

"Can I have the binocular's professor please?" Russell asked.

The land of no horizons

"Of course," Lionel said as he slipped the strap from around his neck and passed them over.

Russell put the glasses to his eyes and made a slight adjustment to the focus. Although he could see them with his naked eye, he was still not quite ready for what he saw through the binoculars. Seven very beautiful women all looking very similar. All of them looked tall with long blond hair down past their shoulders. They were very slim with very fair skin and they were all dressed the same. They were dressed almost the same as Carrie was the first time he saw her. They had a piece of animal skin that came up between their legs and flipped over a string tied around their waists and they had a fur bikini type tops that covered their breasts, he couldn't see anything on their feet. Around their necks they had rough looking necklaces made from shells and colored stones. They all carried long spears. Two of the girls each dragged a pole behind them, stretched between the poles was animal skin and on it was food. There were two large bunches of banana's, some coconuts and other foods that he couldn't see properly.

The land of no horizons

Stuart was tapping Russ on the shoulder waiting a little impatiently for his turn. "Can I have a look please?" He said.

"Ok, here you are," Russell said, reluctantly as he passed the binoculars over to his brother.

A minor adjustment and Stuart had a perfect view of the clearing. He looked in amazement as the girls walked slowly along, not seeming to have a care in the world. It was for him like looking back in time. A first glimpse of an ancient time, when life was much simpler.

"Would you like a look Carrie?" He asked, offering her the binoculars.

"Thanks," she said, as she took the glasses. "These are excellent binoculars aren't they, dad."

"They're much better than mine were," he said. "Pass them over when you're done with them, please my dear."

Carrie passed them to her dad and said, "here you are, daddy,"

The women were close to the center of the clearing now, casually strolling along.

It was the professor that saw it first, a huge

The land of no horizons

snake sliding towards the native girls.

The giant snake was pale in color, it looked like yellow gold, sliding up behind the girls. It probably could smell the small animal that the girls had killed and had on their carrier. Whatever it was that was attracting it put the girls in great danger. This snake was huge at least fifty feet long if not more. Closing in on the girls at a very fast rate.

"Look at that," Lionel said as he passed the glasses to Russell.

Russell put the glasses to his eyes and he shuddered at what he saw.

Stuart almost snatched the binoculars from his brothers hand, as he looked the snake was only a few yards behind the girls and they didn't know it was there. "We have to do something professor, we have to warn them or go and help them."

"We are too far away, they will never hear us if we shout and we shouldn't upset the balance of things down here, remember. Besides that snake may be in big trouble, these women don't back down from anything," Lionel said.

It was Carrie that had the glasses now. She

The land of no horizons

watched in horror as the snake honed in on the girls and their food. Its tongue flashed in and out sensing the food just a few feet away. One of the girls dragging the food was the first to spot the snake. She gave out a scream and let go of the pole she was holding. She turned around to face the snake and brought her spear up in front of her. The other girls all turned around and sprung into action.

The snake raised its massive head and swayed from side to side. This seemed to be a threat, a way to try and intimidate the girls, it didn't work. One of the girls in the back hurled her spear at the oversized reptile. The spear hit the snake in the chest area, the snake recoiled and as it did its tail swished around knocking two of the girls off their feet.

Another of the girls threw her spear at the snake, this one hit it in the face. Again the snake recoiled sharply. Both spears looked like they only just penetrated the skin. The snake reared up and made itself as big as it could. Its whole body swayed as the snake tried to scare the girls away from the food. Both spears fell away as the snake swayed threateningly. One of the girls tried to retrieve her

The land of no horizons

spear, this was a bad mistake. As she got close the snake struck grabbing the girl in its huge mouth. Then in what seemed like a split second it had wrapped her body in three huge coils, tightening, squeezing. The girl screamed as the coils squeezed the air from her body, tightening even more, every time she breathed out, squeezing the life out of her body.

The girls all attacked the snake, poking, prodding, with their spears. The snake seemed to retreat a little then it attacked again. The huge head struck at one of the closer girls but she managed to get her spear in the way and the snake could only succeed in knocking her to the ground. Two of the other girls took this slight advantage they had and got close enough to sink their spears deep into the snake's flesh.

The snake reared up obviously hurt by these two spears penetrating deep into its skin. As the huge reptile recoiled in pain, it loosened its grip on the motionless body wrapped in its coils. As the body slid to the ground three girls charged the snake forcing it back. Two other girls grabbed the

The land of no horizons

motionless body and pulled it away from the snake. The snake was not done yet. It swung its tail section around knocking four of the girls to the ground. In this same motion, it knocked all the food flying in different directions.

As the girls scrambled to their feet and tried to retrieve their spears, the snake grabbed the small Antelope the girls had killed. With the food in its mouth it turned and slithered away as fast as it could. Two girls chased it for a short distance but they soon gave up when they knew it wasn't coming back. Then they returned to the others.

Four girls were on their knees beside the still body lying on the floor. One girl threw her head back and gave out a mighty blood curdling scream, as she acknowledged her dead friend lying in the grass.

Using sign language more than talking they loaded the dead girl on the stretcher that the food had been on. With one girl on each corner they turned back towards the way they had come and headed home.

"Oh my god," Carrie said, "that was horrible,

The land of no horizons

that poor girl, killed protecting a bit of food, was it worth it?"

"I'd bet if they knew the outcome, they would have given up the food. But down here you have to protect what's yours or someone will take it away from you," Lionel said.

"We should go and see if we can help them," Russell said.

"No, we should not interfere,"

" Lionel is right we have to let them live life as if we are not here," Stuart said. No one spoke but it was understood that they would try and have as little contact with the natives as possible.

"Before we go let me show you a couple of other things while we are here. Can you see that ledge up there," Lionel said pointing over to the right, and up the cliff side about two hundred feet? "Well, that's an even better place to watch from. You can see right into the north camp where the men live. And if you look over towards the other side of the cave, you can clearly see a path winding its way up the side of the cave. That levels out a short way up and you can see into the south village.

The land of no horizons

That's where I'm going when we get down from here. I want to see what they do with the body of that poor girl. I have never seen a death like that down here, I'm curious what happens next. If any of you would like to come with me, you are more than welcome?"

"I would love to come with you professor," Russell said. "Are you coming, Stuart?"

"I don't know, do you want to go, Carrie?"

"No, I think I will go and see if I can catch some fish. That will be a change from meat and fruit to eat."

"I'll come with you, if you don't mind?" Stuart said.

"No, I don't mind, it will be nice to have someone to talk to for a change."

The land of no horizons

CHAPTER ELEVEN

Time seems irrelevant when the place where you live has no night. Without the structure of day and night, life changes. When you don't have to get up for work. When there are no weekends, life takes on a whole new meaning. It took Russell and Stuart a few days to get used to this new way of living.

With there being no night there is no special time to sleep. Carrie and the professor were used to it. They would sleep anytime at all. There was no sense of time to it. They would usually sleep twice in a twenty four-hour time period. The clock seemed to have nothing to do with when they slept. It was sometimes ten in the morning when one or the other

The land of no horizons

would go and sleep for as many as five hours. Then sometime later they would go and have a two-hour sleep, it might be two in the morning but it didn't matter. They slept when they were tired, they ate when they were hungry. The rest of the time they would do whatever they wanted.

Collecting food was of course high on their list of things to do, so was collecting firewood. The cave temperature didn't change more than a degree or two, so they didn't need wood to keep them warm, just for cooking. They had torches made of thick pieces of wood, and on the end was some thick gel that looked like glue. This gel would burn for days.

Russell and Stuart tried to fall into this lifestyle, but it was difficult. They had always had very active lives, and to slow down that much was very hard for them. So they both decided to do things that interested them and were beneficial to the group.

Russell had the easier time finding things to do. At home he was quite a handyman. When something broke, or when something needed

The land of no horizons

changing around the house, it was Russell that mum called on to do the job. Behind the house he had a huge workshop, full of all kinds of tools. He had everything that a handyman could want. He had a lathe, a table saw, drill press and cases of drill bits screwdrivers and anything else he could possibly need.

    The tools helped him but he had the skill to use them to perfection. When he cut a piece of wood, it always fit perfectly. They would never call an electrician because if they did Russell would get mad and pout for days, so mum just let him do it in the first place. The biggest project that they did, was to design a huge water garden for the front of the house. Russell and Stuart collaborated on this because Russell needed Stuart to design the filtering system. When it was completed, everyone who saw it thought it was magnificent. It was mums favorite quiet place. She would spend many hours by the waterfall, reading a book, or just enjoying the outdoors.

    The boys often pictured her there when they were away from home. Dad was always at work of

The land of no horizons

course, where else would he be.

Two days had passed since the death of the native girl, and they were sitting on a large rock that overlooked the English Sea, as Lionel called it. The brothers were talking about their mother when Russell had an idea. When the boys were young, they thought that they could send messages to their mother using mental telepathy. This was something they hadn't done for years, but they talked about it and decided to give it a try.

They decided on what to say. Trying to keep it short and to the point. Then they stood up bowed their heads, they held each others hands and said the words.

A Lear Jet was about an hour out from Kennedy Airport, New York. Inside the plane was quiet, there were only two passengers. The man was on the right-hand side of the plane, he was asleep, stretched out over two seats. The woman was looking out of the window at the Atlantic Ocean, many thousands of feet below. Tears ran gently

The land of no horizons

down her face, as she sat reminiscing over her twin boys who she loved so much. Her life now seemed meaningless. They were the glue that held her together, she missed them so much, nothing could ever be the same again.

In Sicily they had done all they could. After talking to the Chief of Police they went to Alondro's house and talked to him. He was very upset, he blamed himself for showing the boys the back road up the mountain. He felt that he should have stopped the boys from going up the mountain when it was so active.

Lawrence explained to Alondro that his boys would have gone up that mountain no matter what he said and that he should not blame himself for whatever happened to them. Then he asked for his help in trying to find them. "I have been told that you know this mountain better than any man on this island and I would like you to co-ordinate the search parties for me. I would like at least three search parties. I want the very best and I will pay top price."

"Sir, you know that the police have already

The land of no horizons

searched the mountain thoroughly, and I believe them when they say that there are no signs of your son's?"

"I know that but they are my sons, and I will not leave here until I have done everything I can. I could not live with myself if we left this place and then I found out that they were alive and we did not find them. I'm sure that you understand, you are a father, would you not do everything in your power if you son was missing like mine are?"

"I will get the best men on the island and we will do everything we can to find your boys."

"Thank you," Lawrence said, as fought back the tears.

Elondro was true to his word he found three teams of very experienced men, women and dogs and he took charge showing them exactly where he wanted them to search.

At the same time Lawrence hired a helicopter. He and Veronica flew around that mountain so many times they lost count.

On the first time around the mountain Veronica knew it was hopeless. This mountain was

The land of no horizons

not like the mountains back home, there were almost no trees, no place to hide, this was a place with no soul, a place that took lives, her sons lives.

Three days later Lawrence called off the search. Except for the dogs finding a bit of a trail there was nothing.

The next day a priest gave a small service on the mountain close to where they found the car.

Now they were on their way home, back to an empty house.

She shook her head in dismay and the tears started to run faster. *I have to break out of this*, she thought and the tears slowed so much that they almost stopped. She took a beep breath and held it there, as she tried to regain control. As she looked over at her husband a voice came into her head, it said, *we are...and we ....come home...day, we are ok....we will.....home someday.* The voice was that of her son Russell and she thought she heard Stuart too. The shock sent tingles down her spine and the hair on her neck stood up. What had she just heard, was this her son's talking to her? Or was this just a grief-stricken mother hoping for a miracle?

The land of no horizons

Should she wake up her husband and tell him what had just happened. No, he would say that she was being silly and she had to get used to the fact that the boys were gone. They had spent almost two weeks in Sicily and they had found nothing. Also, if the boys were ok, why could they not come home now. And why had they not called, they both had cell phones.

She looked out of the window again, not as sad as she was earlier, she knew what she heard, she had heard it before. For now, she just wanted to believe, it gave her something to hold onto. So instead of telling anyone *I will fold it up and hide it in a small place in my heart, and I will keep it safe until my boys come home to me,* she thought.

The brothers looked at each other when they looked up. "Do you think it was ok?" Stuart said.

"I think we did it. Don't ask me why I think it worked, but I think it did."

"Me too. I hope mum got the message, she will be terribly upset."

"I know what you mean," Russell said sadly.

The land of no horizons

"What are you going to do now?"

"We have done all that we can, we have to make the best of our lives down here and that includes collecting food. Carrie said that she was going to get some bananas. I'm going to go with her. What are you going to do?"

"I was going to work on the fence, but the professor wants to go and look in on the south village. He wants to see how they are handling the death of that girl. I should go with him, just to make sure he's ok."

"That was terrible watching that girl die. This place looks like paradise, but it has its dark side too."

As the boys walked back towards the small cave Lionel came striding out of the bushes towards them. "Are you ready to go?" He asked.

"I'm ready and I have the binoculars," Russell said, patting the case on his belt.

"Have you seen Carrie?" Lionel asked.

"She's in the cave. We are going to look for berries and bananas, just as soon as she's ready," Stuart said.

The land of no horizons

"Ok then, we will be off. See you later," Lionel said, as they started off towards the south camp.

Stuart watched them go for a few seconds then he headed towards the small cave that was home for now. The cave was well suited for multiple living, it had a main area about twenty feet around and there were smaller circular pods off that. Lionel had the largest pod, Carrie had the smallest one but her's had another smaller pod off it. There were two other pods left, one was very small and only just high enough to stand up in. The last one was quite big, plenty big enough for the two of them. Inside this cave was dark, so they tried to have a torch burning all the time.

The most unique part of the small cave was that it had running water. The professor had fixed together long pieces of bamboo and tapped into a small stream that comes down the cliff-side behind the cave. The water then comes through the roof and falls from the ceiling into a depression in the floor. There it collects before it runs away outside and finally it ends up in the English Sea.

The land of no horizons

Stuart opened the rickety gate and passed through, closing it behind him. The gate and the fence had been built by the professor without any tools. The fence, is made of twigs, woven together with an occasional post in the soft sand to hold it up. The gate was built the same way, except it had vines as hinges, which didn't work very well.

As Stuart crossed the sand, he could hear Carrie singing. He hadn't heard her sing before, she was a good singer, very good. He walked into the cave to tell her that she was a nice singer but he stopped dead in his tracks. Carrie was taking a shower in the middle of the cave. She was totally naked, standing there, facing him, her head was back as she let the water hit her hair and run away.

Spellbound he could not move, he could only stare. It was only when she stopped singing that he came to his senses and turned around quietly and left.

He left the compound and sat on the rock that looked out towards the island in the English Sea. He sat there waiting for Carrie to come out of the cave. Had she seen him, did she sense that he was there?

The land of no horizons

He could not get the sight of her beautiful naked body out of his mind, nor did he want to. But he was ashamed of himself for being in that situation. He now remembered Lionel saying, that when you take a shower, you have to sing so that others will know not to come in. He had forgotten, and now he felt very guilty. His only hope was that she did not know that he was there.

As soon as she came out of the cave, he knew he was in trouble. She came marching over towards where he was sitting. Wearing only the goat skin top and shorts. Her hair wet and scraggly sticking to her face, she looked gorgeous. He tried to look at the sand at his feet but he couldn't. The smoothness of her motion, was so sensual, he wanted to take her in his arms and hold her. He wanted to tell her how sorry he was but he couldn't. As she got closer, he could tell she was mad.

"Did you come in the cave while I was showering?" She said.

"Well er, yes I did."

"You do remember my dad telling you not to come in if I was singing loudly."

The land of no horizons

"I had forgotten."

"Forgotten, you expect me to believe that."

"Well, it's the truth. I had forgot and I'm very sorry please forgive me, it will never happen again, honest."

"You can bet your life it will never happen again," she said as she seemed to run out of things to say. She stomped her feet turned around and marched away. As she did a little smile crossed her lips, why she didn't know.

Russell and the professor were scrambling up a steep narrow path that took them high above the south village, where the women lived. It was a slow climb as the path was all lose rock and some care had to be taken or they could easily slide down the steep side to the valley floor. When they got to their vantage point, they sat on the path with their feet hanging over the side. The path at this point was slightly wider than lower down, and it was also flatter and it was solid rock.

Russell took the binoculars out of their pouch and passed them over to Lionel. "Thank you my

The land of no horizons

boy," he said as he put them to his eyes. This is a great spot to watch the village, even without the binocular's Russell could see everything that was going on.

The village was made up of fourteen huts mainly in a circle around the outside of the clearing, there were two larger huts inside the circle. The huts were almost identical, built of straw and twigs woven together. Then the lower half was wrapped in very large green leaves. Just above the leaves was open, with only the posts that held up the thatched roof showing. The thatched roof' were also covered in those very large green leaves, overlapping each other to keep the rain out.

"Professor, have you noticed the very large openings to let the light into the huts. As it never goes dark here, whenever they sleep they don't seek out darkness like we do. Do you find that a little strange?"

"I did at first but then the more I thought about it the more I understood them. We are used to the dark and we accept it. These people have not really seen it. The only place we have found

The land of no horizons

darkness down here is in our cave. I think that's the main reason that we are allowed to have the cave is that they don't want it, they are probably scared of it. If you were like most kids the dark frightened you a bit, well these people are in some ways like children. They have not progressed as far as we have yet, we all have some fear of the unknown, the dark, don't we."

"I guess you're right, professor."

"Would you like to use the glasses?"

"Yes please," Russell said as he reached for the binoculars. Scanning the village he noticed something he had missed before, under a tree that was almost dead center of the village was what looked like a stretcher raised up on four polls. On the stretcher wrapped in a white cloth sheet with green leaves patterned into it, was the body of the girl that had died. Her head was the only visible part of her body.

When Lionel and Russell had come over earlier, there had been no sign of the body. Now it was wrapped ready for something. Were they going to bury it, or was there another plan?

The land of no horizons

"Did you see the body under the tree?" Russell asked.

"I did. Have you noticed how the other girls act when they pass the body?"

"No, I haven't. What do they do?"

"Watch and you will see."

Russell watched, but non of the girls were near the body. Then one came out of one of the huts that was closer to the middle of the village. She looked a little older than the other girls that he had seen. She was dressed a little different from the others. She had on the same top as the others but instead of the loin cloth type bottom, she had on what looked like a skirt. It was very similar to some that natives wear in Hawaii and Fiji.

As she got close to where the body was she dropped down on her knees and she approached the body that way. When the rest of the girls saw this they also moved towards the body and when they got close, they also dropped to their knees. Only the first women approached the body.

"I think she's the queen," Lionel said. "Whenever I see her, she seems to be in charge."

The land of no horizons

"Could she be a witch doctor or something like that?"

"Maybe, but I have never seen them doing anything like that. No charms, or portions, nothing like that. But whenever she is around the others seem to look to her for guidance. I think she is very beautiful, do you agree?"

"She is. She has the look of a Marilyn Monro. What's her name, do you know?"

"I haven't got a clue. They don't talk very much, they do most of their communication by sign language. Watch them and you will see, it is very interesting."

Russell watched closely. The queen had moved right up to the head of the corpse. She was looking down the body. She very slowly raised her hands and placed them on each side of the face of the dead girl. Then she lowered her head, so that her forehead touched the forehead of the corpse. She stood there quietly for a long moment. The whole village was motionless. Until the queen raised her head and stepped back. At that moment four of the girls stood up and walked over to the stretcher, with

The land of no horizons

one girl on each corner they stood their waiting.

The queen slowly raised her arms and when they touched over her head the four girls picked up the stretcher. The queen turned around and started to walk away. As she did so, all the girls stood up and following the stretcher, the procession followed the queen.

"Where do you think they are going professor?"

"I'm not sure, but if I had to guess I would say they are probably going to the Grand Canal. And if we are quick, we can beat them there, and see how this ends."

Stuart was not sure what he was going to say but he had to try and do something, he didn't like Carrie being mad at him. He desperately wanted Carrie to like him, he wanted her to be his friend and he had just done the inexcusable. As he walked over towards the cave, he tried to think of what he was going to say. But all he could do was think about her beautiful naked body standing in that shower and the water cascading all over her.

The land of no horizons

As he got close to the cave entrance, he could see Carrie sitting quietly on the floor of the cave.

"What can I say to make things better?" He asked.

"Nothing."

"I'm really sorry. I honestly forgot what your dad told us. Will you forgive me please?"

Carrie said nothing, she just stared at the sand.

"If you want you can see me naked, to make us even, that's ok with me?" He said, as he started to take his shirt off.

"No, please, no, not that," Carrie said laughing. "Please keep you clothes on, there has been enough nakedness around here for one day."

"Then will you forgive me."

"I don't know about that, I haven't decided yet."

Stuart sat down at the side of her and said, "your friendship is the most important thing in the world to me, I wouldn't do anything to jeopardize that, honestly. Please, lets try and forget that this happened and go and see what we can find for dinner." Stuart stood up and held his hand down so

The land of no horizons

that he could help Carrie up. She hesitated for a few seconds, then she reached up and grabbed his hand. He gently pulled her to her feet and as she stood there almost nose to nose, he desperately wanted to hold her in his arms and kiss her. But he thought, he'd better not. He looked deeply into her beautiful blue eyes and thought he saw the same longing that he had.

"Ok, if we are going to look for food we should get going," Carrie said, as she moved away.

"I'm with you, what are we looking for today?"

Lionel and Russell had a lot of ground to make up if they wanted to get to the Grand Canal first. The women had a much shorter distance to go but they had a body to carry and that would slow them down considerably.

Both men were a little out of breath, when they got to the ledge that overlooked the canal. There was no sign of the women, if they were coming to this spot then the men had made good time.

The land of no horizons

They sat on the edge of the overhang, watching, hoping that they had come to the right spot. Although this was a sad time, it was also interesting to watch how a primitive race of people handle death. Would it be much different from how it is in America, or Britan? They had to wait and see.

Just as they were beginning to think that they had come to the wrong place, they heard the women coming. They were chanting and stamping their feet. This was not what the professor had expected at all. They don't normally speak much, yet here they are chanting at the tops of their voices. The words or chants didn't mean anything to the professor. He listened to see if they could be words that he might decipher some day. The sound was a happy sound, it was as if they were trying to make it a happy send off.

When they got to the edge of the canal, they placed the body on the small outcrop, that the professor had said they used to sacrifice the men. As soon as the body was placed on the ground, all the women started to dance. They jumped around like children who were trying to make up a new dance.

The land of no horizons

Then the queen started to dance. She had been stood at the back of the group waiting quietly. Her dance seemed to have structure, she waved her arms and shoulders and swung her hips. She moved in a very seductive way. Almost like a belly dancer but not so intense. All the other women sat down where they were and went quiet.

The queen swayed back and forth as she was slowly getting closer to the body. Finally, she was stood by the head of the corps. Her dancing had slowed almost too a stop. Slowly she sank to her knees, then she leaned forward until her forehead was touching the forehead of the corpse. She stayed there for a second or two, before she raised herself, looked at the body and stood up. As she walked away from the body, she placed a hand on the head of one of the other women.

This younger woman, danced almost the same dance as the queen and when she had finished, she placed her hand on one of the others and the dance started again.

Finally when all the dancers were done, the first four dancers slowly walk over to the stretcher.

The land of no horizons
They stood there for a long second, then they lifted the back end of the stretcher and the body slid into the flowing lava of the Grand Canal.

    Carrie was an expert at climbing trees. She could climb faster than anybody Stuart had ever seen. It was as if she was part monkey the way she scampered up to the tops of the trees. Once she was up there, she would throw down the fruit and Stuart would collect it. As the day wore on he felt better about the way that things were between the two of them, she seemed to have been able to put it out of her mind, even though he never could.

The land of no horizons

CHAPTER ELEVEN

Over the past few years Lionel and Carrie had lost all contact with time. They had no watches there was no night-time no way to keep track of time. The result was that they would eat at any time and sleep when they were tired. Now that the twins were here things started to change, gradually a little bit at a time.

Without any real attempt to alter their lifestyle, this is what was happening. The first thing that seemed to happen naturally was that the main meal of the day was usually eaten around five thirty p.m. This was always followed by sitting around and lots of talking. The professor was a very interesting

The land of no horizons

man he had traveled most of the world and the stories he told were fascinating.

Of course the boys had stories to tell also. There were the big things that were going on. They told them the tragic story of 9/11 and the terrible loss of life. There were of course the consequences of that act. The sending of troops to Afghanistan and the war in Iraq. Lionel listened, he said very little, he just shook his head in disbelief.

It became that the evening chats as they got called, was the hi-light of the day.

Everyone had something interesting to add to the conversation. The boys explained how they are twins yet they don't look a lot alike. "Mum was having problems conceiving." Stuart said, " so she took fertility pills but they didn't work. So she went and had what was a new procedure at the time, were they take eggs from the mother and sperm from the father, put them together in a special dish, then they replace them back into the mother. Mum had four eggs inserted into her, two survived."

"So, we are twins. Russell is older than me by about eight minutes. He has mums looks and he has

The land of no horizons

dads build. I look more like dad but a smaller version."

It was Russell who told them about the movie star mum and the millionaire dad.

"Your mum must be devastated at losing you two, with no other children. I feel sorry for her," Carrie said.

"I'm sure she is very upset but on the bright side just think how happy she will be when we get out of here," Stuart said. "What about your mother she must be missing you?"

"No, my mum is dead, she died of cancer about two years before we moved to Africa. One of the reasons that we moved was to get away from the memories."

"I'm sorry to here that," Stuart said. "Cancer is a hard way to lose anyone you love."

Russell had taken on the job of handy man. He felt that he should try and improve the look and the feel of the camp. He had a few tools to work with. In their backpacks they had a few things they could use. Probably the best tool was a small campers axe,

The land of no horizons

they also had a folding shovel, plus they each had Swiss army knives. Of course with their climbing gear they had nylon rope, pitons, hammers. So although they didn't have a lot, what they had was useful.

The rope was not to be used, everyone agreed that the rope should be saved in case they needed it to get out of here. Most of the other tools could be used many times but once you cut the rope it loses some of its usefulness. So the rope was safely put away for when they needed it.

With Stuart's help Russell fixed the gate, improved and extended the fence. Lionel had done a good job of the fence considering he had no tools. But Russell built hit higher and stronger. He also started on his biggest project. One of the things he wanted to do was to build a raft so they could try and visit the island. This was a big job but with everyone helping and under Russell's stewardship they all felt that it was possible, with a lot of hard work.

Russell was also working on something else but he wouldn't tell anyone what it was. It was his

The land of no horizons

secret and he told no one, not even Stuart.

Lionel was happier now that the boys were there, they helped keep Carrie occupied. He would feel guilty leaving her alone at the camp. But he so wanted to study both groups of natives. Now he could. Carrie now always had someone with her. Stuart was almost always there and sometimes Russell too.

At first he was a little worried that the boys might take advantage of Carrie, being that she was very naive about how things are with boys and girls. So one of the first things that he did was talk to the boys. He confided in them, he told them about his concerns and to his delight they assured him that nothing would happen between them. As he got to know the boys better he believed them but he did sense a growing romance between Stuart and Carrie. This worried him a bit but he decided nature would take its course and the best thing he could do was to stand by and let it happen.

Besides helping everyone Stuart had his own little talent. He was a good artist. Back home he dabbled in oil painting, mainly seascapes. Along the

The land of no horizons

California coast there were many beautiful places that he could sit and paint and this he did whenever the mood took him.

Here in this strange land of no horizons, he had no oil paints but Carrie had some drawing paper and some colored pencils. When Lionel saw how good an artist he was, he asked him if he could draw some of the unusual animals that roamed around. Stuart was delighted, it gave him something he could do to contribute to the team.

Whenever Stuart and Carrie went out to look for food, the sketch pad went with them. Life was lived at a casual pace. If they saw an animal of interest, they would stop for as long as it took to draw it. Then they would continue with what they were doing.

It was on one of these days when they were just out looking for berries, that they spotted him. They had crossed the stream and were heading towards the cliff face when Carrie saw him. The Saber-Toothed Tiger. He was siting in a small clearing alongside the stream. As Stuart and Carrie closed in on him he didn't seem to notice them. It

The land of no horizons

was only when they got close that they could see why. He had just made a kill. He had in his paws a small deer, that he was leisurely eating.

This was a perfect time to draw this magnificent beast. Slowly they moved to a suitable position where they could see him and hopefully he would not see them. It took Stuart almost an hour to get the likeness that he wanted. Feeling very pleased with his work, they quietly moved away and let the animal finish his meal.

When they got back to camp, Carrie rushed over to show her dad the drawing. "What do you think of that dad?" She asked.

"Oh, that is masterful. It capture's the raw savagery of the the animal. People will defiantly believe these animals exist when they see these drawings. You do great work Stuart, great work."

"Thank's professor, I'm glad you like them."

"Like them, I love them. Let me go and show these to your brother," he said, as he went looking for Russell.

As Carrie went over to sit at the table a tall black man stepped out of the bush. He stopped for a

The land of no horizons

second look when he saw Stuart, then he did a double take when he saw Russell come out of the cave with the professor.

"Jo Jo its good to see you. Come on over let me introduce you to some new friends."

The land of no horizons

CHAPTER TWELVE

The dinner that they all sat down to was the best one the brothers had tasted in a long, long time. Jo Jo had brought back some turkey meat that he had cooked, along with some fish that he had smoked in a way that brought out all the flavor. When they mixed this with the fresh fruit and berries that Carrie and Stuart had collected, it was a wonderful meal. Finally there was the conversation and laughter to complete a great day.

Jo Jo was a very interesting man. He had traveled all over Africa and he had searched the valley from one corner to the other trying to find a way out. But without any luck. Back on the surface Jo Jo had a wife and two kids that he desperately

The land of no horizons

wanted to see. This was the driving force that kept him going. He hoped he could find that passage that would lead back to his home and family.

He told stories of caves that he found but he was unable to explore them as much as he wanted to. He made torches out of tree branches, straw and vines. But they only lasted a short time not long enough to explore them properly. He could not carry the sap that they used at the camp. One of the first things he asked was did they have flashlights, and he was very disappointed when they said no.

They sat around for hours talking, telling stories about life on the surface. How things were changing not always for the better. It was two a.m. when people started to head for their beds. This had been an amazing day, Jo Jo was quite a character.

It was Russell who was the last one up, this had become a kind of standing joke that whoever was last one up, had to clean up after the morning meal. It was a little unusual for everyone to be sat down at the same time for the early meal but today they were.

The land of no horizons

Jo Jo was very interested in the raft that they were building. He said he thought that the best chance of finding a way back, was across the sea. He had searched the valley without any luck, so sailing across to the island seemed the most likely way to find a way back home.

Everyone seemed to agree and so with a more concentrated effort they all pitched in and worked on the raft. Jo Jo was a big help, he could find things that the others couldn't. Up to now they had collected logs and not much else.

They had two nice logs they had decided would be the main supports that the raft would be built on. Then other logs were dragged out of the forest and laid on top. Some were niched out to get a better fit but most just sat on top of the main supports. The one thing they lacked was a way to tie them together. If they had to they would use the nylon ropes that they had. But they had promised themselves, that they would only use them as a last resort.

Jo Jo said that he knew where there was a lot of vines that could be used to strap everything

The land of no horizons

together. They worked very hard on the raft for the next few days. Jo Jo left to find those vines that he promised. The others scoured the jungle looking for suitable logs to use. Finding them, trimming them and dragging them back to camp was slow laborious work.

After days of long hours and hard work the watches said it was Sunday. So everyone agreed to have a rest day. Lionel decided he would go and watch the north camp for a few hours. He hadn't spent much time watching the mens camp, so he said that's what he would do. Jo Jo thought that sounded like a great idea and said he would go with him.

Russell said he would go and work on his secret project and he disappeared into the jungle. Carrie said that she was going for a shower and gave Stuart a stern look that told him to keep out.

"I think I will go for a swim in the sea, I haven't been swimming for a long time. Why don't you come with me it will be fun?" He said to Carrie.

"No, I think I'll have my shower," Carrie said as she turned and headed towards the cave.

Stuart shrugged his shoulders and he started

The land of no horizons

off down the beach. The water was warm, like the tropical fish tank he had at home or like the ocean around Hawaii. He looked around and as there was no one looking, he took off all his clothes and waded right in.

The water was great. He had forgotten how much he enjoyed swimming. The water was crystal clear and as he dived under the water he was amazed at how many fish he saw. They were mainly small fish, some of which he recognized from his days working in the pet shops. He couldn't believe his luck, this was like a little piece of heaven for him. To be able to swim in such pristine water and watch the fish. This is going to be one of my new greatest pleasures he thought.

As he surfaced for about the twentieth time, he checked his position, he was about fifty yards from the beach, not far for a good swimmer like him. He trod water for a few minutes catching his breath, breathing deep.

He looked around still no one on the beach, he didn't care he was having fun. He took a deep breath and dove under. A few strong stokes and he was

The land of no horizons

about fifteen feet down. There was a large rock cluster to his right with what seemed like hundreds of fish swimming around. A shift of his body and a kick of his legs and he was heading that way. Just to his left was a jellyfish. It was small about three inches across. It was beautiful, red with small flourescent green dots. He reached out to touch it but he drew his hand back at the last second, realizing that things down here aren't always as harmless as they seem.

    He turned away and headed for the surface. He had not seen the giant jellyfish that was ten feet away and two feet below the surface. As he headed up for a breath of air, his legs rubbed against the fifteen feet long tentacles that trailed behind it.

    The pain was instant and intense, it seemed to suck the strength out of his body. Instead of going up he felt like he was going down. Using his arms he paddled as strong as he could, he tried to kick his legs but he couldn't feel them, if they were working he couldn't tell. The pain shot all the way up his spine into his head and even into his eyes. He was sure that he was going to die.

The land of no horizons

As he looked up, he realized that he was only a couple of feet down. He could see the waves breaking just above his head. Using only his arms he broke the surface. His head cleared the water and he took a deep breath. Another deep agonizing pain spasm shot up his back and settled in his shoulders. The pain was so strong it made it difficult to breath. His legs now felt like a dead weight, dragging him down below the waves.

It took every bit of strength that he had to get his head above the water. He sucked in more air and this seemed to trigger another set of shooting pains all through his body. He was very weak now, he hardly had the strength to breath. He thought he heard a sound a voice "hold on, I'm coming for you," it seemed to say. Now everywhere was going dark, water was going into his mouth. He closed his lips tight as he slipped under the water.

At first he couldn't feel the hands that were pushing him up to where he could breath again. Only when his face broke through the waves and he spit out water and sucked in air did he think that he had a chance to live.

The land of no horizons

"Breathe, Stu breathe," the voice said.

He tried but it was painful, he could only take small sharp breaths. The hands under his armpits felt good, the body close to his, kicking hard. "Can you kick your legs or paddle your arms?" The voice said.

Moving his legs was just too painful. He tried paddling with his arms and he could manage that a little. They must be close to the beach because he could feel himself being dragged and finally dropped in a few inches of water. He looked up and there was Carrie looking very concerned, staring down at him.

"What happened, are you all right?"

"A jelly fish, I think," he said in a week voice.

"I should go and get my dad he can help."

"No, stay here please. It will take too long to get your dad. I think I'll be ok, just give me some time."

Carrie kneeled by his head and brushed the sand out of his hair and started to cry.

"Why are you crying, you saved my life again, please don't cry?"

Carrie wiped her eyes but said nothing.

The land of no horizons

Stuart could feel tingling in his toes and his breathing was getting better. He could move his right leg a little it was then that he remembered that he was naked. He didn't know what to do, he still couldn't move. He was too far away from his clothes to reach over to them.

Carrie had pulled herself together and she said, "are you feeling better now?"

"I think things are improving, slowly, I can feel both feet and one of my legs."

"Good, If I bring your clothes over do you think you can put your shorts on?"

"Er, yes I think I can, just pass them over" he said feeling very embarrassed.

Carrie stood up and walked the short distance to where his clothes were. She picked up his shorts and threw them over to him. Then she turned around so she wouldn't see him put them on.

"It's ok now, you can look I'm not naked anymore."

"Thank god for that," she said. As she made her way back to Stuart. "Do you always swim with no clothes on?"

The land of no horizons

"No, it's just that I didn't want to get my shorts wet and there was no one around, so I thought it would be ok. The pain was slowly ebbing out of his body and the strength in his legs was returning. "My legs feel better now, I think I can stand if you will help me?" he said.

"Are you sure you're ready? We can wait a few more minutes if you want to."

"No, I'm ready. Just help me up please."

With Carrie's help he struggled to his feet. But his legs still weren't strong enough to hold his body up. Carrie caught him and put his arm around her shoulders. "Let me help you," she said.

"Ok, thanks, my legs are not as strong as I thought they were," he said, as he let some of his weight rest on Carrie's shoulders.

"I've got you. Lets just go slowly over to the table. We can sit there till you feel your back to normal."

"Ok, lets just go slow, I don't want us to fall down again," he said, feeling a little guilty using Carrie this way but enjoying every second of it.

* * *

The land of no horizons

Lionel and Jo Jo sat quietly just watching the inhabitants of the north camp go about there daily business. The men did very little of anything, the few women that were there did all the work.

Four men sat on some rocks talking, using mostly hand signals. One of them indicated that he wanted one of the women to come over to him. She seemed reluctant to go over but he yelled at her and she went over. When she got there he grabbed her arm and pulled her down to the floor. She struggled a bit but he hit her and she stopped. The men all laughed at her. One man pushed her over with his foot and they laughed harder.

The girl snarled at them but that made them laugh even more. The first man indicated that she should leave, as she got up to walk away he tripped her up and she fell face first into the dirt. She jumped to her feet and turned quickly ready to attack the man. Before she could do anything all four men stood up and stared at the girl. She knew that she couldn't beat all four of them and if she did the others would get her and beat her. Then they would beat her son, so she walked slowly away and

The land of no horizons

the men laughed some more.

"These men are terrible to their women aren't they?" Lionel said.

"It wouldn't surprise me if the women slit their throats while they were sleeping. If I treated my wife like that I know I wouldn't wake up the next day."

"Why do men act like that, is it something very primitive in all of us?"

"I don't know professor but it's a trait we could live without."

Jo Jo had the binoculars and he passed them back to Lionel, as he did he lay back against the rock and looked down the valley as far as the eye could see there were trees, some with flowers. It was as he was relaxing that he noticed something in the distance, at the far end of the cave, something strange.

"Can I have the glasses back when your done with them?" Jo Jo asked.

Lionel passed them back without saying a word. Jo Jo took the glasses put them to his eyes and adjusted them slightly.

The land of no horizons

"What are you looking at?" Lionel said, looking down the valley in the direction Jo Jo was looking.

"I'm not sure what it is," he said apprehensively. "There's something unusual going on way down there, can you see it."

"Not without the binoculars I can't. What are talking about."

"Ops, sorry professor, here take a look. Just to the right of that very large tree at the far end of the cave."

"Ok, I can't see anything" Lionel hesitated. " Do you mean those two trees that look like they've lost all their leaves?"

"Exactly those two trees. They weren't like that a few days ago."

"Are *you sure*?"

"Yes, well I'm pretty sure, I was just down there."

"What should we do about it?"

"I'll go and check it out. The last thing we need is something coming at us and we don't know what it is."

The land of no horizons

"Your right of course, any idea what it might be?"

"No, none. My guess if I had to make one, would be insects of some kind. It could be locust or something like that. But I'm just guessing, I should head out right away and find out for sure."

"You don't mean right now do you?" Lionel said sounding very concerned.

"No, I can wait until tomorrow."

The land of no horizons

CHAPTER THIRTEEN

"What were you and dad doing all day?" Carrie asked.

"Not much, just spying on the neighbors. I have to go and collect some supplies. I'm leaving in the morning," Jo Jo said.

"*Leaving*, already, but you only just got back. Do you have to go so soon?" Carrie asked.

Russell was siting on a rock a short distance from the camp. He had no idea how close his brother had come to drowning. He was putting the final touches to his secret project. It felt good in his hand, if it worked as good as it felt, then it would be time well spent. It was ready, time to head back to camp

The land of no horizons

and show everyone.

Lionel and Jo Jo were collecting the bits and pieces that Jo Jo needed for his little trip, when Russell walked out of the jungle carrying his latest creation. He was very pleased with himself, he hoped that it would be a benefit to everyone even though he would probably be the one to use it. As he closed in on the others sitting around the table, it was Lionel that spoke the first.

"Ah ah, so that's what you have been working on, a bow and arrow. That's a great idea. Have you tried it out yet?"

"No, I was scared I would lose one of the arrows in the bush, I thought I would wait until I got back here to try it."

"Go on then Russ, let's see how good of a shot you are," Stuart said.

Everyone turned to watch as Russell pulled one of the arrows from the quiver he had made. The arrow looked nice and straight, he had used bright blue feathers as flights. Russell took his time as he fitted the notch in the tail of the arrow onto the bow

The land of no horizons

string. Then he very deliberately raised the bow with his left arm straight and his right hand holding the arrow in place. Everyone was silent as Russell drew back on the bow string so that the arrow was level with his right eye.

As soon as he released the arrow it was obvious it was not going to work properly. The arrow wobbled twisted and fell to the ground about ten feet from where it started.

Everyone started to laugh, especially Russell. This was the funniest thing that they had seen in a long time. "That worked well," Russell said. As soon as he stopped laughing.

"I think you need some modifications," Stuart said.

"I knew that would happen," Russell said.

"You know what the problem is don't you," Lionel said.

"Yes, they need a tip on them to add weight to the front," Russell said.

"Of course they do. Pass one over and let me take a look at it." Lionel said.

Russ passed over one arrow then he

The land of no horizons

said,"Where are we going to find something like that down here?"

"Oh, I think I might be able to help there. Bring the arrows and your tools I have an idea," Lionel said. "Come with me I have something I want to show you."

Russell smiled as he picked up the rest of the arrows and followed the professor.

" I have to go in the morning but I will only be gone for a couple of days," Jo Jo said.

"What's so important that you have to leave so soon?" Stuart asked.

"Its nothing important, its just something I have to do," Jo Jo said looking very uncomfortable. "I'll be back soon, just a few more things I need, but before I go I want to talk to you."

"Sure Jo Jo what can I do for you?"

"Lets walk down the beach I have a little story I want to tell you."

Stuart stood up from the bench and slowly the two men started to walk away from the compound.

"This story I'm going to tell you is for only you to hear and I don't want you to repeat it to

The land of no horizons

anyone is that clear?"

"Ok," Stuart replied sounding a little concerned.

"About four month's before we arrived in this place we were in my village. There were the three of us and at that time and Carrie was only nine. This one day it was a very warm day and the boys in the village were playing football on some spare ground just outside the village. Carrie being the tomboy that she was, was also playing."

"She always played with the boys and most of the time she was the best player on both teams. No one ever watched them play there was no danger and when they were finished they all went to there own huts."

"This day the game had been finished for a while and Carrie hadn't come back to where me and Lionel was sitting. So I started to look for her. I soon found her in one of the huts. Five of the boys had taken her in there and taken her clothes off and two of the older boys had taken their clothes off too."

"When I found them, I was mad, I made

The land of no horizons

Carrie get dressed and I sent her to meet her dad. When she was gone, I beat those boys. I made each one sit and watch me beat the others. When I was finished, I threatened them and told them that if they ever did that again to any girl, I would hunt them down and I would peel the skin from their feet. They ran home terrified of me and what I might do to them."

"Carrie was alright but I think it upset her and she never trusted boys the same after that. The reason that I'm telling you this story is, to tell you that I love that girl as much as I love my own two girls. And I don't want anything to happen to her. The other reason is that I sense you have real feelings for her and I wonder if what happened when she was nine still affects the way she feels about men."

"I think I understand a little better now," Stuart said. "Thank's for telling me that story, it clears things up considerably."

"I want it clearly understood that I don't want anything to happen to Carrie or I will be so mad I don't know what I'll do," Jo Jo said.

The land of no horizons

Stuart didn't speak for a second or two then he said, "do you mean me? Do you think that I'm going to hurt her?" He said angrily. "NOW LET ME TELL YOU SOMETHING, SHE HAS NOTHING TO FEAR FROM ME. I WILL DO EVERYTHING I CAN TO PROTECT HER FROM WHATEVER THIS PLACE TRIES TO DO TO HER." he yelled.

The big black man put his hands gently on Stuart's shoulders and said, "that's the kind of response I was hoping for. I know now that you love her and that I have nothing to fear, I will leave her safely in your hands." Jo Jo held out his hand and shook Stuart's hand, then he started to walk back towards the small cave.

Carrie came running over and said, "what was all that about, you shouting at Jo Jo?"

"It's ok, just a small misunderstanding but it's all cleared up now."

Carrie was still puzzled but she didn't say anything.

"Well I think its strange that he's leaving so soon, he usually stays around for about a week or more. I hope everything's all right."

The land of no horizons
"I'm sure it is, your dad would have told us if there was any danger. What would you like to do now?"

"What do you think about trying to making a crab trap? If we can, we might be able to have fresh crab with our late meal tonight."

The land of no horizons

CHAPTER FOURTEEN

The professor and Russell had plans for their day. They wanted to put the finishing touch on the arrows that Russell had made. Stuart decided to tag along, he was curious as to what they were going to use to use to make the tips out of. It felt strange to Carrie being alone. Since the boys came she had never been alone there was always someone there. She sat and thought what could she do, but she couldn't think of anything interesting. After she tidied up she took off after the men to see what they were up to.

Lionel was not only an intelligent man he was

The land of no horizons

resourceful. His keen eyes missed nothing. So when Russell needed help with the arrows it was only naturel that Lionel would be the one to help. During his years in this strange land he had walked most of the trails that the animals made and on one of these occasion he spotted something very interesting. Laced into the cliff wall along one small part of this giant cave he noticed a vain of silver material. Scraping at this metal with his knife, he flaked off some high grade silver.

    This was what he planned to use as tips for the arrows. Silver was not the best metal that could be used as arrow tips but when it's the only thing you have, you have to try it. Silver has quite a high melting point, so the plan was simple. Build a fire underneath the vain in the wall and hope for the best.

    Underneath the vain in the cave wall they made a slight hollow in the soft soil to build a fire in. They were hoping that heat from the fire would rise and melt the silver allowing it to drip out of the rock.

    Russell had made a mold out of clay and with

The land of no horizons

a bit of luck he hoped it would work. All they had to do was get the silver out of the rock and into the mold. They had wanted to start yesterday but decided against it. Lionel had pointed out that it would take many hours to get the silver hot enough to melt, so they delayed the start until today, this way they could get an early start. There was the definite possibility that it would take all day but they were prepared for that.

With the fire going, the men just sat around waiting to see what would happen.

It was about half an hour later that Carrie showed up.

"How did you find us my dear?" Lionel asked.

"It wasn't hard, I had an idea where you were going and when I got close I could smell the fire."

"Sit down, join us. The boys were telling me about their grandfather and how he started Barron Pharmaceuticals."

"I'd love to dad but I was planning on going to get some vines to use on the raft and I could use some help....."

"I'll come with you," Stuart said, cutting

The land of no horizons

Carrie off.

"I *can* go on my own, if you want to stay here," Carrie said coyly.

"Let Stuart go with you, I would feel better if you had someone with you just in case something happens."

"Daddy we have lived down here for nine years, I think I can look after myself. But if Stuart wants to come we'll be able to carry more vines and that will be better for me."

"I'd love to come, you just lead the way. See you guys later," Stuart said.

As they left the small clearing Russell said, "I think we have a real romance growing there."

"Hmm yes," Lionel replied, not sounding sure if it was a good thing or not.

It was a long walk to where the best vines were. Jo Jo had shown them where to go and which vines to select. They wanted to get the strongest and the most supple. There was no rush. Time was not a priority in the land of no horizons. Carrie and Russell just dawdled along, taking their time

The land of no horizons

enjoying each others company.

The path they were on went past the lagoon where Stuart had dropped into this strange world. This was one of their favorite spots. They would come here just to sit and talk, happy to be together. The water was pristine and the place a mini paradise.

"Why don't we rest for a while?" Stuart said.

"Ok."

The beach was pure white sand like you would expect to find on a tropical island. Just up from the beach was a large area of grass, it was nice and flat here and this is where they sat down.

They had only been there for a short time when Stuart said "Lets go for a swim."

"Now, are you sure. The last two times you went swimming you almost drowned?"

"This time I want you with me, to protect me. You know, to look after me."

"Ok, but you have to keep your shorts on. No nude swimming."

"Ok, lets go."

Carrie was wearing the shorts and T shirt that

The land of no horizons

he had given her. She took off the shirt first then the shorts. Underneath, she still wore the animal skins similar to the ones she had on when they arrived. Stuart couldn't take his eyes off her as she ran towards the water. "Come on slowpoke it was your idea to go for a swim. *Lets go.*"

"I'm coming," Stuart said as he took of his shirt and shoes. Then he ran after her. As he got close, she screamed and dove under the water. He immediately did the same, following her grabbing her ankle and pulling her back. She kicked hard and broke clear and started for the surface. He followed trying to catch her but she was too fast for him. He surfaced a couple of feet from where she was. She looked at him gave a little laugh, leaned back in the water slowly kicking her feet, she started to move away.

They played in the water until they started to get tired then they swam to the side and lay down on the soft sand. Russell propped himself up on one elbow so that he could look at her. She was so beautiful lying there. The little bit of clothing she had on clung to her body, leaving very little to the

The land of no horizons

imagination. Her eyes were closed, her long hair looked bedraggled. But she could not look more beautiful if she tried.

He leaned over and kissed her gently on the lips. Her eyes shot open as he pulled away. "What are you doing?" She asked.

"You looked so beautiful I had to kiss you," he said, very embarrassed.

She jumped to her feet and hurriedly put her clothes on. "Did I ask you to kiss me?"

"Er no, I just thought you wanted me to."

"Well, I didn't."

"Why was it not nice?" He asked, as he put his shirt on.

"Just cause it was nice, didn't mean I wanted you too."

"Oh, so you did like it then."

Carrie was flustered she didn't know what to say. Stuart put his hand on her arm and gently pulled her close. Then he kissed her passionately. She seemed to melt into his arms as he held her body close to his.

" I don't think we should do this," she said in

The land of no horizons

a whisper as their lips parted. She gently pushed herself clear of him turned around and walked away. He smiled and started after her. "Are you mad at me?" He asked as they walked side by side through the jungle.

"No" she replied in a sharp tone.

"Please don't be mad at me."

"I'm not mad at you but my dad would be if he saw us, kissing."

"I'll tell him."

"*No, don't please,* it will make things worse if you tell him, please don't say nothing, *please.*"

Stuart stepped in front of Carrie and she stopped and looked into his eyes. "Carrie, I think, no, I know that I'm falling in love with you. And if your dad, doesn't like it there is nothing he can do about it. I just hope that you have similar feelings for me too."

"I do have feelings for you, I just don't know what those feelings are. You are very special to me and I enjoy us being together. But I'm not sure that its love."

"It is, but you are unsure and that's ok. The

The land of no horizons

only thing I ask is not to fight it, let it come slowly, naturally and when you're ready I will be here standing next to you, ok."

"Ok."

"Now lets go and collect some vines."

Russell and Lionel were sitting by the fire chatting away as if they had known each other for years. The rock face was getting very hot but as yet the silver refused to melt.

Lionel was interested in the Barron family and how they had developed the business. He was also very interested in how new technologies were advancing the treatment of complex diseases. Russell was happy to talk about his work, especially to the professor. Lionel listened intently soaking in information like his brain was a sponge. This is how you become a smart man Russell thought.

The two men had been enjoying themselves, just idle chatter, but very interesting. Then it happened the first drip of silver dropped into the mold. At first it went unnoticed, then Russell saw the second droplet land in the mold.

The land of no horizons

"Professor, it working, I just saw some silver drip into our mold?"

"Really, that's brilliant," Lionel said as he scrambled to his feet.

Russell was looking at the few droplets of silver on the bottom the mold when Lionel got there.

"Look at that its working, I was beginning to think it wasn't going to work." Three more drips quickly dropped into the mold.

"Get your arrow ready we have to do this while the silver is still hot."

Russell went quickly over to his quiver and took out his first arrow.

Stuart and Carrie had been working for hours searching out the best vines. Then cutting them into as long a length as they could. Now they had lots. Perhaps too much.

"Do you think we can carry all this back to our camp?" Russell asked.

"You just read my mind, I was just thinking the same thing. Perhaps we should leave some here, it's a long walk back and there's no sense in trying

The land of no horizons

to carry too much."

"We can put some under those bushes and cover them with leaves."

"Stu, we are not in America now, no one will come along and steal them."

Stuart thought for a second then he started to laugh, "for a second there I'd forgotten where we are."

"I'm hungry, do you want to start back now?" Carrie said.

"Yeah, let's, I'm starving." He picked up two moderate size bundles of vines and started off towards home. Carrie also picked two bundles of vines and she started off after him.

Russell was ecstatic at how the arrows had worked out. Now that the silver was cold, it felt like the tips were on better than he hoped. He had tried a few trial shots and he was impressed as to how well they flew. A bow and arrow were not new to Russell, he was a member of the local archery club back home. The bow and arrows that he made were not as good as the one's he had at home but he was

The land of no horizons

very pleased with how it turned out.

This bow was more like the ones that Robin Hood would have used not like the three bows that he had back home. His other bows were competition bows. He had belonged to an archery club for more than ten years and in that time he had become most proficient with a bow and arrow. Of the three bows he owned, he liked his newest one the best. It was a precision instrument with a very good set of sights. He had improved tremendously since he bought the new bow.

The Black Arrow Club he belonged to was one of the best in the country and was famous in archery circles. Throughout the year they would have competitions with other clubs in the area. At the end of the year the best club was presented with a trophy, his club had won it eight out of the past ten years.

The competition to get onto the team was intense. Russell had never quiet made the team but he had been first alternate a few times. He tried very hard to make the team but he just couldn't quite get there. So he practiced every chance he got.

The land of no horizons
      *   *   *

Before they started heading back to camp they had stoked up the fire and put half a coconut shell under the silver vain, in the hope they could catch some more.

It would take them at least forty-five minute to walk back to camp, so they put all the arrows in the quiver and started back towards home.

"I'm very grateful professor, using the silver like that was an excellent idea, I will see if I can make some more arrows and we can go back tomorrow and put tips on them."

"I think we will find many uses for that bow and arrow. We need a good way to get coconuts down from the trees and for hunting it will also come in handy.

The two men were happy as they made their way along the jungle paths heading back towards camp. Just as they got to the large clearing, there in front of them was Stuart and Carrie. Looking down at something on the ground. From where they were stood it was too far to tell what they were looking at.

Russell was just about to shout to them when

The land of no horizons

he noticed a small movement in the grass. At first it was hard to tell what it was, its shape and coloring seemed to blend almost perfectly with the grass and shadows. It was moving slowly, closing in on them. Chills ran down Russell's spine when he realized what it was. His brother and Carrie were in mortal danger. The big cat was only twenty yards behind them, and it was slowly stalking them, moving silently.

Lionel had not seen the Saber-Toothed Tiger blending into the surroundings as well as it did. Russell pointed in the direction of the big cat. When Lionel did see it, his blood ran cold. This was his biggest fear that something would come along and take his baby girl away from him.

As the Tiger closed slowly on the unsuspecting couple, Russell could see what a magnificent animal it was. A killing machine, in perfect condition. Its muscles tense as it closed in, ready to pounce on its unsuspecting prey. The big cat rose up slightly in the grass. This was it, he was about to attack.

Russell's voice broke the silence just as the cat

The land of no horizons
started its run, *"STUART LOOK BEHIND YOU,"*

Stuart and Carrie both turned around, they could sense the panic in Russell's voice. What they saw terrified them. There charging at them was the king of this jungle, the Saber-Toothed Tiger. He was only a few yards away running at full speed towards them. Carrie who was stood a couple of feet behind Stuart, was now closer to the big cat. Stuart reached out took her arm and pulled her behind him.

When he had seen the cat before he had not realized how big it was or how powerful he was. At full speed every muscle in its body was working and what a powerful beast it was. Stuart could not believe that even now, in the last couple of seconds in his life he was in awe of the animal that was going to kill him. It was no more than three strides away from them closing in on them with every split second and there was absolutely nothing he could do. One more stride and it would be on top of them. Then just as its front feet hit the ground before its final spring the big cat's head twisted violently away from them. The whole body of the tiger shuddered as it moved sideways falling into the long grass.

The land of no horizons

When it hit the ground, it rolled over landing on its side sliding through the grass.

Stuart and Carrie watched dumbstruck as the big cat scrambled to its feet, looked at them with a cold stare then turned and ran away.

As the Tiger was closing in on Stuart and Carrie, Russell had acted quickly. He had drawn an arrow from his quiver, slid it against the bowstring drew back on the bow and let fly. The tiger was ready to spring as the arrow got close but he could not see if it hit. What he did see, was the cat tumble away falling heavily into the grass, then springing to its feet and running away.

Russell looked at Lionel and said, "what happened?"

"I don't know, I honestly don't know," he replied.

"Let's go and see if they are ok," and he started to run to where his brother stood.

"Stuart, are you all right?"

"Yes, I'm ok, Carrie are you ok?"

"I think so," Carrie said in a shaky voice.

The land of no horizons

"What happened, one second he was almost on top of us then he fell down, then he got up and ran away. Why in gods' name did he not kill us."

The two brothers looked at each other and shook their heads in disbelief at what had just happened.

Lionel arrived a little out of breath, " are you all right my dear, I thought I was going to lose you," he said, sounding like he was trying not to cry.

"I'm fine dad," Carrie said, as she walked over to him and gave him a hug.

Lionel took her in his arms and gave her a long squeeze, not wanting to let her go.

Stuart saw something in the grass and he walked over to retrieve it. As he bent down to pick up the arrow, he noticed something else lying in the dirt, close to the arrow. He picked it up and examined it. Then a small smile crossed his face.

"I think I know what happened," he said, as he got back to the others.

"I'm glad you do because I'm totally mystified by it all," Russell said.

"It's simple really, when you shot that arrow

The land of no horizons

at him you hit him on one of those fangs."

"In the tooth?" Russell asked, "how do you know that?"

Stuart raised up his hand and between his thumb and first finger, was a piece of something about an inch long, hard and white. Russell held out his hand and Stuart dropped whatever it was into it. Then Lionel and Carrie came over for a look. Lying in Russell's hand was the tip off one of the fangs from the Tiger.

"That's incredible, talk about a million to one shot, that's it," Lionel said. Russell turned it over in his hand and just looked at it, there was a look of total disbelief on his face.

"Well Russ, you are the only person in the world to have a piece of a tooth from a Saber-Toothed Tiger, how does it feel?" Stuart said.

"I guess that it's something special, I'm just happy everyone's all right including the Tiger. I'm glad he didn't get badly hurt, or worse, killed. In the end I'm happy because it could have been a lot worse."

"*Your right*, I could be dead and what would

The land of no horizons

you have told mum when you got back. She would have killed you for not looking after me." Everyone laughed and the tension was lifted. "Also think of the story you'll have to tell at the archery club next time you go."

"I won't be able to tell this story no one will believe me."

"What were you looking at before the Tiger attacked, you seemed to be totally enthralled in whatever it was?" Lionel asked.

"Enthralled, is the wrong word, disgusted is a better word. Come over here and look at this," Carrie said. She took a couple of steps from where they were stood and pointed at something lying on the ground.

"That's what we were looking at," she said.

Russell was the first one there, followed a second later by Lionel. "Oh, that's disgusting what is it?"Lionel said. As he looked at the half-eaten carcass lying on the ground.

"That's what we were trying to figure out. It doesn't look like a deer and it's not an antelope, no horns, so what is it?" Carrie said.

The land of no horizons

"If I was to make a guess I would say it's a dog or a wolf, or something like that," Russell said.

"That's what I was thinking. We couldn't decide what it was but I thought it looked a bit like a dog," Stuart said.

"Anyway now we know why old chip tooth attacked, he thought you were going to steel his kill. He was protecting his food," Lionel said.

"He can have it," Carrie said, "it looks disgusting to me."

"Let's get out of here so chip-tooth can come and have his dinner," Stuart said.

"Pass me some of those vines little brother, you look like you brought too many."

Just as they were ready to walk away Russell stopped and listened, "did you hear something?" he asked.

"No, I didn't," Lionel said.

"Nor me, what kind of noise was it?" Carrie asked.

"I don't know it wa...... there it is again, did you hear it that time."

Everyone shook their heads. Then there was

The land of no horizons

a sound, a very faint sound coming from the bushes. Russell moved slowly towards where he thought the sound was coming from. He looked but he couldn't see anything. He was just about to give up when he heard it again. He pushed his way into the bushes and out of sight from the others. A few seconds later he returned carrying something under his shirt.

"What's that you've got there?" Carrie asked.

He carefully pulled it from under his shirt and said, "it's a puppy!"

The land of no horizons

CHAPTER FIFTEEN

"A puppy let me see" Carrie screamed excitedly, as everyone crowded around.

"That's amazing," Lionel said as he looked at the pup. "How old do you think it is?"

"I don't know, Stuart is the animal expert in our family, what do you think?"

"Can I hold him for a second?" Stuart asked.

"Sure thing, take it. See, I don't even know if it's a boy or a girl," Russell said as he passed over the puppy.

Stuart gently took the puppy from his brother and looked into it's eyes. The puppy was a good size, a big ball of fur, mostly grey in color, with a little bit of white on its nose and toes. It was almost

The land of no horizons

too big to be held in one hand. Stuart placed his finger in the puppy's mouth to feel for teeth.

"His eyes are open and he has no teeth so that should put him about three to four-week's old. And it is a boy, that's for sure."

"Can I hold him?" Carrie asked. She took him from Stuart and hugged him gently. "Isn't he the cutest thing you ever did see?"

"He is a handsome pup," Lionel said. "What are you going to do with him, Russ?"

"I don't know, what do you guys think? Can we risk leaving him here? If we do, will he end up like that carcase over there? I think that might be his mother. I think she tried to stand up to old chip-tooth and she lost that battle."

"You could very well be right," Lionel said. "And if we leave him here and the big cat doesn't get him, there's a good chance he will starve to death. Unless his mother is hiding somewhere, waiting to come and get him as soon as we are gone."

"I think we should take him with us, the risk is just too great. The Tiger will come for his dinner

The land of no horizons

and hear him whimpering and that will be the end of him," Russell said.

"We have to take him, it's the only thing we can do," Carrie said.

"He really needs his mother's milk, he's a bit too young to eat solid food. We do have goats milk, I guess that might do," Stuart added.

"So we all agree that he should come home with us?" Russell asked.

Everyone nodded their heads. "Ok, lets go home," Russell said.

That night the puppy was a big problem. He didn't want to drink the goat's milk, he missed his mother as he whined all night. It was only when Russell picked him up and put him in his bed that he settled down and slept for a few hours.

The next morning he drank a bit more milk and he seemed happier after that.

"I hope he doesn't whine like that every night," Lionel said in a sleepy voice.

"No, he won't daddy, he's going to be a good boy, aren't you little one," Carrie said, as she held

The land of no horizons

him close to her face and looked into his eyes. "Have you thought of a name for him yet, Russ?"

"I was thinking of calling him lucky but then I changed my mind. I think I will call him Wolf. Partly because he might be a Wolf and even if he isn't he will be a big dog, and that name suits a big dog. What do you guys think?"

"I think Wolf is a grand name," Lionel said

"Me to," Carrie chirped in, passing him back to Russell.

"I like it too," Stuart said.

"Then it's settled, Wolf it is," Russell said happily, as he put the puppy on the ground.

Wolf, tried to stand and did so for a few minutes. Then he slowly started to walk away.

"You will have to keep an eye on him or he will disappear into the jungle," Stuart said.

"I will, don't worry," Russell replied.

It had been three days since they had found the puppy. He was doing better every day. He walked with only a small hesitation in his step and he also tried to run. Everyone thought that this was

The land of no horizons

the funniest thing. He would run a few steps, then he would stop or just fall on his face. Then he would get up and do it again. Each time he did it, he would get a little further.

Russell had spent all his time with Wolf, they had sat on the beach. Spent some time running around and Russell had called his name lots, trying to bond with the puppy, trying to get him used to being around people. It seemed to be working.

Stuart and Carrie were off somewhere collecting food for the main meal of the day. Lionel had disappeared early, without a word to anyone about where he was going.

It was a nice change for Russell to stay around the compound. He had fed the goats, and cleaned up a bit while Wolf slept.

Carrie and Stuart were the first ones back, carrying fruits and coconuts.

"Do you know where Lionel is, I haven't seen him all day?"Russell said.

"I saw him early this morning, but he didn't say where he was going. He gets secretive some times, he will be gone for days. This time I think he

The land of no horizons

is up to something, we will find out what it is when he's good and ready," Carrie said.

"How's Wolf been today?" Stuart asked.

"He's been great. He will sometimes come when I call him and he is trying to run more. I might try and see if he can eat a little bit of meat today. What do you think, will it be ok?"

"You will have to chew it up a bit for him but he should be trying to eat a bit of solid food now." Stuart replied

"Ok then, I will try him when we have our evening meal."

Carrie had just put out all the food when Lionel came striding into the compound.

"Where have you been all day?" Carrie asked.

"I had something I wanted to finish, and now I've done it," he said.

Carrie looked around and couldn't see anything new, so she said, "don't keep us in suspense, tell us what it is?"

Lionel dipped his hand into the pocket of his raged shorts and pulled out something small and passed it over to Russell. "I hope you like it?" He

The land of no horizons

said.

Russell took it, looked at it and with a big smile on his face he said "I love it, thanks a lot Lionel, that's excellent." Russell held it up so everyone could see. Lionel had taken the piece of tooth that had chipped of the tiger and instead of there being a rough end, Lionel had capped it in silver. Then he had fashioned a loop and attached that to the silver cap. Finally he had threaded a long thin piece of leather through the loop.

"That's very nice, put it on," Stuart said.

"Nice work daddy, how did you do that?"

"It wasn't hard to do, I'm glad you like it."

"I *do* like it, but if you don't mind, I would like to give it to my brother. What he did the other day, when he put himself between that big cat and Carrie, that was one of the bravest things I have ever seen, and I would like for him to have this, if you don't mind professor?"

"That's a very fine gesture and I don't mind at all."

Before Stuart could say anything, Russell put the leather necklace around his brothers neck and let

The land of no horizons

it drop.

"I don't know what to say, it is very nice, thanks a lot," Stuart said, sounding a little embarrassed.

"That's ok Stuart, it looks great on you," Russell said.

"Yes Stuart, I agree it looks great," Carrie said.

"Well now that we are all here, let's eat," Stuart said trying to change the subject.

"I'm starving" Lionel said, "I haven't eaten all day."

The land of no horizons

CHAPTER SIXTEEN

In California the sun was shining, it was a beautiful day. The hills that overlook Sacramento were magnificent this time of year, there had been some rain and cooler weather so the grass was green and the trees full of foliage. The Barron house was resplendent, the gardens truly magnificent, full of flowers, shrubs and trees.

Around the back of the house were two very large tents. Inside the first tent was food, lots of food. The second tent was set up with tables and a bar. Both of these tents were beautifully decorated, lots of white Orchids and red Roses.

There had been lots of arguments in the Barron house over today. Veronica didn't want it at

The land of no horizons

all but Lawrence insisted. Being the pragmatist that he is, he wanted to have funeral service for his sons. Even without their bodies he needed to put them to rest. He felt that enough time had passed and that it was the best thing for everyone.

Veronica said that if he wanted to do that he could, but she wouldn't go. She believed that her sons were still alive and would come home some day. This Lawrence found very disturbing, he thought that she needed to let go of this fantasy and realize that her sons were dead and that they were not coming back, ever.

After much arguing they compromised, it was decided that they would have a ceremony. But there would be no coffins. The ceremony would be a celebration of the lives of her sons. The priest from their church would come and oversee the service, and there would be prayer's and hymns. The important thing was that it was not to be morbid, it was to be upbeat and a happy occasion.

Although Lawrence was not happy about the way Veronica wanted to do this, it was the only way that he could get her to attend, so he gave in and let

The land of no horizons

her do it her way. Their marriage had lasted longer than most because they would compromise, they talked things through and each gave a little. In the end they each got a part of what they wanted and life went on.

They were both getting dressed for the ceremony. At first Veronica had put on a pale yellow dress and a white jacket. This lead to another argument, in the end she put on a black skirt and jacket and a bright orange blouse. Lawrence wasn't totally happy but he kept quiet. He put on a dark blue three piece suit and a pale blue shirt and a black tie.

Soon there would be two hundred and fifty people arriving some of which would be VIP's. Most would be from Barron Enterprises and it's subsidiary company's but there would also be a large number of personal friends of the two boys. Veronica had also invited lots of her personal friends and some of their neighbors, it was going to be quite a party.

The service lasted a little over an hour then

The land of no horizons

everyone headed for the tents. Veronica was the perfect hostess, she was happy laughing, talking to everyone in turn. Lawrence and most of the top-ranking company executives had gone into the house for brandy and cigars.

Inside the large drawing room, people sat around sipping nervously on their brandy. Until now Russell and Stuart's jobs had not been filled but now the expectation was that Lawrence would make the necessary changes soon. No one expected him to do it today but they all wanted to be seen and be around just in case he did.

Lawrence had invited all his top executives and everyone showed up, none of them dared miss this, one of them flew in from Europe to be there. There was also a lot of up and coming managers and minor executives there, all waiting to hear if Lawrence would give any indication of what he was thinking. He didn't disappoint them.

In his quiet voice he told them that there was going to be major changes in the way the company was run. He didn't elaborate but everyone tingled with excitement at the thought of major changes,

The land of no horizons

how would that affect them.

"Listen everyone I have some serious thinking to do why don't you all go and join the party and I will be out there shortly," Lawrence said.

Slowly they picked up their drinks and headed outside. A few of the higher executives touched Lawrence's shoulder as they passed by him. The whole company was ripe with gossip about what was going to happen with the company.

Lawrence had been advised many times to turn the company into a public company. It was worth millions on the stock market and all the top executives knew this. If Lawrence decided to go this route, it could mean millions of dollars to all the executives and top managers. The opportunity to buy shares before they hit the market or even better to get some free shares, had everyone in executive positions on edge.

The only reason Lawrence had refused to make the company public was that he wanted his sons to take over from him and take it to the next level. Now that the boy's were gone, would he decide to take the company public?

The land of no horizons

Alone with his thought's Lawrence realized this was a very sad day for him and Veronica. This was the day that all his dreams for the company died. He had worked so hard and sacrificed so much with the hope that his boys would carry on the business, now those dreams were dashed. He had risked his marriage, now he planned to try and rebuild that relationship even if he had to leave the company to do it.

With the boys gone life had lost a lot of it's meaning. Although he had never told them, they were what he drew on for inspiration in everything he did. The business was theirs just for the asking, he dreamt of the day that he would step down and let his son's run things, but that dream was dashed. Why had they gone to Sicily, why had they climbed that volcano, why had they died?

Tears started to run down his cheeks, without his boys what was the point of carrying on. Lawrence was an only child, he had no other family, now it was just him and Veronica, life for them would never be the same again.

He knew how much it was affecting him, it

The land of no horizons

was affecting Veronica more. She would not accept that they were not coming home, and he had to be close at hand when she finally realized that there was no hope and she would never see them again.

Outside the party was starting to get going, the booze was flowing and the food was delicious. In one corner was a DJ playing quiet appropriate music. Veronica was talking to her good friend Carol-Ann and some of her other friends.

"This is turning out better than I had expected," she said.

"It is, the food is fantastic and can you believe how many people are here. It's a wonderful turn out for your boys," Carol-Ann replied. "They would have loved it."

'Your right wait till I tell them what they missed they will be really mad," Veronica said. "Excuse me girls I have just seen an old friend and I must go and say hello to him. I will be back soon."

Veronica rushed away disappearing into the crowd.

"Do you think she's ok, she's supposed to be

The land of no horizons

in tears at her sons memorial? Instead it's like she's at the biggest garden party that she's ever given," her friend Joan said.

"I know what you're saying, I was worried about her so I talked to Lawrence, and he told me that she is seeing Dr Hampton the psychiatrists. He's the best, it's very hard to get into see him he's so busy. Lawrence had to pull lots of strings to get him to see her."

"I've heard that he's very good, and he's very expensive, but they can afford it."

At first Veronica refused to go and see a shrink, she knew that she was not crazy. But the more she thought about it, the more she started to like the idea. She couldn't tell her husband what happened on the plane. There was absolutely no way that she could tell her friends that her boys had sent her a telepathic message. They would say that she was crazy. So who could she talk to? She could talk to a psychiatrist, he couldn't tell Lawrence anything. So she thought about it, then she decided to go and see him and it has been better than she expected.

The land of no horizons

With each session she had opened up a bit more and now she was totally relaxed around him.

His office is in one of the most fashionable parts of town in a hi-rise tower that looks like it should be in a magazine. In the foyer is a waterfall that drops from about fifty feet into a pond full of fish. Around the pond are beautiful tropical plants and marble statues of Angels and ancient Gods.

Dr Hampton's office was just as spectacular as the foyer, with washed oak book shelves and desk and leather chairs. On the wall were paintings, landscapes, most of which looked like originals.

From the first time she saw him she liked him. He's a handsome man with a kind smile and a soft voice. He's the kind of man that I could have an affair with she thought, if I was that kind of a person. The best thing about him is that he listens to her and he doesn't judge her.

Her first visit was a two hour session. She told him all about her boys. How they were conceived, how she had a difficult birth with them and all about their childhood. She made sure to tell him about the telepathic messages that they sent her, even when

The land of no horizons

they were young. She asked him if he had heard of twins being able to do that and to her surprise he said, "yes, there had been many claims of telepathy between twins and some between a mother and her twins."

Now that she had set the seed she continued with her story. She talked about how they loved to live on the edge. They would always try new things, like hang gliding, they loved snow boarding and their craving for adventure.

Finally she told him about the ill-fated trip to Sicily, and how the car was found but not the boys. She told him about Lawrence, how he did everything he could to try and find the boys but with no luck. Then she told him what she had been leading up too all through this session. She told him about the message that she got from them while she was on the plane. She watched him nervously as she said the words, he didn't show any emotion at all. What the hell was he thinking, she couldn't tell.

When she had brought him right up to today she stopped and looked into his eyes looking for some kind of reaction, she didn't get it.

The land of no horizons

After a few seconds he looked up at her and asked the question that she dreaded, "if your boys aren't dead where are they and why haven't they called you?"

The question was very blunt but it was a question that she had asked herself at least a thousand times, and couldn't find an answer to. She thought for a second or two and as tears filled her eyes, she said, "I don't know, this is the biggest question. I do know that if they could, they would call me, so wherever they are there are no phones. At first I thought that they could have been kidnaped but in their message they said that they were ok. If they had been kidnaped, they would have said so. But they didn't. So doctor I can't answer that one, I wish I could."

When Veronica left that beautiful office she did so with a heavy heart. She took the elevator to the underground parking. Her car was parked close to the elevator, she opened the door and sat in. It was a warm day and the car was warm even though it had been parked underground. She turned on the engine and waited for the air-conditioning to start to

The land of no horizons

work.

      While she sat there she thought about the visit. He had asked the question that hurt the most, "why had they not called?" He said. "You know that there is nowhere on this planet that doesn't have phones, so why have they not called?"

" I wish I could answer that one, I would go there and get them," she said to herself.

      She thought about that few seconds on the plane when she heard their voices. *I wasn't asleep, I wasn't dreaming in any way, the voices jumped into my thoughts without any warning. And it was my boys. It happened just like when they were young. I know it was them, I just know it. The words were not clear but I understood them and that's all I need.*

      Now that she had that clear in her mind she was happy again, she backed the car out of its parking spot and started towards home.

The land of no horizons

CHAPTER SEVENTEEN

Lionel was in his favorite place, he was sitting on the ledge overlooking the south village. He couldn't decide if he was a scientist or a peeping tom. As a scientist this was an incredible opportunity to study a race of people that no one in the outside world had ever seen. Not only were they beautiful, they were top of the pecking order down here. This gave them a confidence that they carried with them wherever they went.

The thing that Lionel liked the most was that they were always happy. If Lionel ever felt sad or unhappy, he would come here and watch the women in this village. They had a tremendous amount of

The land of no horizons

energy, a lot of which they put into being happy. This was especially noticeable around the children.

If the kids were playing a game, it was normal for the adults to join in and the kids welcomed them. They played a game of tag but with their own rules, where if they were touching another player they could not be tagged. They also played a hunting game. They all got their spears and sneaked around in the bush, then they would rush out and throw their spears at a dead log that was leaned up against a tree. If they hit it and their spears stuck in, then they all gave a big cheer, if the kids missed then they got a second shot, if the adults missed they got jeered. Lionel had watched them play this game many times but he only just realized that their spears stuck into a hard piece of wood. This posed the question what were they using for a tip? He had never got a close look at one of their spears but now he wished he could, were they using silver like he had, or was there something else available?

They played their games for hours, everyone having fun. The way that they lived their lives was very communal. Everyone did their part, they all

The land of no horizons

looked after the kids, they all prepared food. It was a simple life but a happy and fulfilling one.

One thing that they did a lot of was hugging, it seemed that every chance they got, they would hug each other. They did this mostly with the kids, but the adults hugged also, it was very touching to watch.

Both the adults and the kids seemed to go into whichever hut they wanted to, it was difficult for Lionel to keep track of them. He had tried in the past to document which child belonged to which adult, but he had to given that up as an impossible task. The more that he watched the village the more sure he became that the kids didn't know which adult was their birth mother. At first this was a hard concept to get his mind around. Knowing how western women look after their children, it was hard to believe that these women could treat each child as if she gave birth to it, but they did. There was no favoritism shown, all the kids were treated exactly the same.

He was sure that the adults knew which kid was theirs even if they didn't show it. He wondered

The land of no horizons

how the next queen would be picked, was this something passed from mother to daughter, or was there another way of deciding who would become the next queen? They had lived this way for thousands of years so there must be a way to pick a new queen.

For a long time he had wondered if the men and women had ever lived together, and if they had what had made them split into two different groups? It was always assumed that the men were the stronger and more dominant of the species but not here. Here the women were definitely more dominant, the men stayed clear of the women at all times, and if their paths did cross it is always the men that backed down.

For a scientist like himself this was an unbelievable opportunity, but if he ever escaped from this place he could not disclose his findings. If he did, others would come and that he could not allow. As a scientist he had to do everything in his power to protect this land of no horizons from the outside world.

Today he had Russell's binoculars with him so

The land of no horizons

he could get a closer look at what was going on below him. The village life was like normal, everyone was milling around doing what they needed to do. Kids were playing games, and the adults were preparing food for the next meal.

About half a mile behind the village there was a large open area with a small hill on the side closest to him. Into this clearing came four figures, two adults and two teenage girls. They must have been out collecting food because they were carrying a small deer that they had killed, as well as some fruits. As they made their way across the clearing, the big saber-tooth tiger entered the clearing at the other side. From where he was he couldn't see them and they couldn't see him.

The small group of women started up the hill from one side, as the tiger started up from the other. It was obvious that they were going to meet when they got close to the top. Lionel thought about yelling some kind of warning but he knew it was useless, they wouldn't understand what he was saying, even if they could hear him.

With the binoculars firmly planted against his

The land of no horizons

eyes he watched, fascinated. The people reached the top of the hill first. When they saw the big cat, they stopped but instead of readying their spears they placed the sharp end on the ground and casually leaned against it. When the two girls saw this, they did exactly the same.

The tiger was only about ten feet away from them when he spotted them. He stopped in his tracks and crouched back on his haunches, looking at them with those big gold eyes. It would only take him a couple of seconds and he would be on top of them. But from his body language that was not going to happen.

It was a stare down, the people with a fresh kill that the cat would like, but weren't prepared to give up, against the king of the jungle.

It only lasted a few seconds then the cat turned and skulked away disappearing into the jungle.

The adults said something to the girls and then they started again towards the village.

Lionel breathed a huge sigh of relief, it was fascinating to him as he watched these simple but happy people. They had everything they wanted,

The land of no horizons
there was plenty of food and water, lots of space and the best thing was that they were the dominant species. From Lionel's perspective they had just about everything they could want.

The land of no horizons

CHAPTER EIGHTEEN

Russell was up early the next day, Wolf had been whining so much that he took him outside to give him some goat's milk and a little bit of meat. He lapped up the milk out of a coconut shell, then he chewed at the dried meat. Russell stayed close so that he could make sure that the puppy didn't choke on the meat.

Although Wolf had only been with them for a few days there was a strong bond developing between Russell and him. When he was awake, he would follow Russ wherever he went. When Russell sat down he would curl up at his feet and go to sleep. If Russell got up and moved away Wolf

The land of no horizons

would almost certainly wake up and followed a few steps behind. Sometimes Russ would sneak away without awakening him, then he would watch from a short distance away when the puppy woke up. Initially the pup would look around, wondering where Russ was, then when he spotted him he would run over wagging his tail, looking as happy as a puppy could be.

After about an hour of playtime Wolf was sitting on the beach chewing on a piece of stick. Lionel had just got up and was sitting at the table.

"I would love a cup of tea," Lionel said. "Just a nice cup of tea and a scone. I would like to be sitting in one of those outside café's in London enjoying a nice mid-morning snack."

"I know how you feel, I used to like to sit out in our back garden and have a large cup of coffee, sometimes mum would join me. We would sit there and not say much, but it was a special time that I miss."

Carrie was the next one to sit down at the table. She looked like she should have stayed in bed for another hour but she said that she was awake and

The land of no horizons

she could hear them talking, so she decided to get up.

The three of them just sat at the table talking. Stuart joined them after about half an hour, bringing out some food for everyone. As everyone picked at the fruit and dried fish something in the distance caught Carrie's eye.

"What's that?" She said, pointing to something flying over the island.

They all turned to take a look at what Carrie was pointing at. Circling over the island, was what at first looked like a huge bird. It was just gliding like a vulture circling it's pray. But it was too big to be a vulture, the body part was large and the beak was out of proportion. Instead of the beak being short and hooked it was long and pointed, not like any bird that any of them had seen before.

"I'll go and get the binoculars, then we might be able to tell what it is," Russell said, as he got up from the table and walked quickly towards the small cave.

"What do you think it is professor? It doesn't look like a bird to me?" Start said.

The land of no horizons

"My eyesight isn't as good as it used to be, I can't see it very well," he said as he squinted his eyes trying to get a clearer look.

Before Russell could return with the binoculars, the creature disappeared behind some trees on the island.

"Where is it?" Russell said as he emerged from the cave. "It's gone. You took too long, it went behind those tall trees on the left side of the island," Stuart said.

"Don't worry it will probably come back in a few minutes," Carrie said. "Come and eat, before we eat it all."

Russell reluctantly went back to the table and placed the binoculars next to where he was sitting.

Before Russell could put any food in his mouth, it was back again climbing into the dome above the English Sea. It had a very unusual wing motion, it was not like a bird it was more like a bat. The wings seemed to beat slowly but they had tremendous movement. The wings almost touched at the top and bottom of each flap, making it look like it was doing it in slow motion.

The land of no horizons

No one spoke as the creature flew to the top of the dome then slowly headed towards the beach area where they were all seated. As the creature got closer, it became obvious what it was, but at first no one spoke, it was too hard to believe.

"It's a pterodactyl" Stuart exclaimed. "Can you see that, it's a pterodactyl?"

"I see it, I see it," Carrie screamed.

"Aren't they related to the dinosaurs?" Russell asked.

"They sure are, they were around at the same time." Lionel said.

They all just stood there mesmerized, watching as this link to the great dinosaurs, slowly flew to the highest point in the smaller dome, then glided around making huge circles over the sea.

Russell had the binoculars and he used them for short time then he passed them off, and Lionel used them. He then passed them to Carrie so that she could get a better look. Finally Stuart got his hands on them, so that he got a closer look.

The body was large and lumpy not smooth like a bird. It was hard to tell what the skin was like

The land of no horizons

from this distance but he thought it looked like hair not scaly like a reptiles. It was difficult to estimate the size but the body had to be at least six feet long. Then there was the head with its crocodilian like snout. Inside that mouth were teeth, in rows, sharp like shark teeth. The wings were huge about fifteen feet across, looking like bat wings, leathery.

"No one has seen this creature for millions of years, thought to be extinct but here is one and where there is one, there has to be more." Stuart said.

After about ten minutes of circling it flew back towards the island and disappeared.

"That was truly remarkable," Lionel said.

"That's a bit of an understatement dad, we have just seen a flying dinosaur. A real flying dinosaur!"

Everyone sat back down at the table, for a few seconds no one spoke, they all wanted to re-live what had just happened.

"Amazing, is the only word that I can think of to express what I just saw," Stuart said, letting out a big sigh.

The land of no horizons

They were all so immersed in their conversation that they didn't see the pterodactyl skim the top of the trees on the island, and drop to about six feet above the waves over the English Sea. With a few powerful strokes of its wings, it hit hi-speed heading towards the beach.

It was closing in fast when again Carrie noticed it. "It's coming back, look."

They all turned to look in the direction, that Carrie was looking. And sure enough, there it was, skimming the surface of the water. Closing in on them at a tremendous speed. At first everyone was happy to get a closer look at such an unusual animal but there was a menace about the creature, it had a purpose. It was as if they all saw at the same time what the pterodactyl was after. Russell was the first to react he leapt to his feet and yelled, "wolf, look out."

Wolf looked around at the sound of his name and he stood up. He took two steps towards Russell who was running as fast as he could towards the pup.

The pterodactyl swooped the last few feet and

The land of no horizons

in one smooth move grabbed Wolf in its mighty jaws and shook him, hard. Russell was only a few feet away as he tried in desperation to stop what was inevitable. He threw himself towards the fleeing reptile but he was too late. He landed face first in the sand and as he looked up he saw the pterodactyl clear the trees and start to climb towards the high point of the large dome, Wolf lying lifeless in its jaws.

Russell's head dropped to the sand, as he fought back the tears.

"Russ, are you all right?" Stuart asked as he caught up to his brother.

There was no answer. Russell had just lost his new friend. Wolf had only been with them for a short time but he had found his way into the hearts of all of them. But it was Russ who had found him. It was Russ who fed him and looked after him. Now Russ had let him down and the pup had paid the ultimate price.

Carrie was the next one to arrive, "oh my god, oh my god, poor Wolf," she said with tears streaming down her cheeks. Lionel arrived a few

The land of no horizons

second later, unable to speak after what he just saw.

Russell was still face down in the sand but the other three watched as the pterodactyl circled back towards the island and then it did something that caught them by surprise. Instead of flying back to the island, it landed on a shelf high above the English Sea. The shelf didn't appear to be very large as the creature perched on the edge with its back to them. Then after only a second or two, it turned and flew off heading away from the island towards the main cave. Wolf was not in its mouth, it had dropped Wolf on the shelf, probably to pick up later and take him back to wherever it came from.

No one spoke for a few minutes then Lionel said, " I think I might be a bit too optimistic but there is a slight chance, that Wolf might still be alive."

"What makes you think that?" Carrie said.

"Well, when that creature first dropped Wolf on that shelf, I could see his paw with the binoculars, but now I can't."

"Are you sure, professor?" Stuart said.

"Oh I'm positive, his paw was sticking out

The land of no horizons

where I could see it. Now it's gone. We know that there aren't any pterodactyl's living on that shelf, so it is possible that he is still alive."

"Can I look, professor?"Stuart said.

Lionel passed over the binoculars. Stuart placed them against his eyes and made a slight adjustment. "I can't see a foot or anything," he said.

Russell was now sat up on the sand looking towards the shelf. Stuart passed the glasses down to Russell. "Are you telling me that Wolf is on that ledge?"

"Yes, that thing dropped him there and then flew off down the main cave," Stuart said.

"I'm going to get him. Alive or dead I don't want that monster to feed on him," Russ said.

"That looks like a tough climb are you sure you can do it?" Lionel said.

"We've climbed harder than that, haven't we, Stuart."

"We have. I'll go and get the gear, I'm coming with you."

"No, no gear, and I'm going alone. I need you to stay here, this has to be a quick climb. There will

The land of no horizons

be no time for safety gear, all that I'm going to take is our long piece of rope. When I get up there, I'll tie the rope around Wolf and drop him down to you. You will have to swim out and get him and bring him back here."

"I don't like it, you going up there on your own."

Russell put his hand on his brother's shoulder and said, "you know it's the fastest way if I go on my own. Will you go and get me the rope please, while I study the climb?"

This was Russell's usual way that he started a difficult climb. He would plan the best route before he started. When he had the route in his head then he would go.

Stuart came running back with the rope. "Are you absolutely positive you don't want me to come with you?"

"Positive. Stay here and watch my back for me. That thing might come back again." Russell took the rope from Stuart, he lifted it over his head passed his right arm through it and he let it sit on his shoulder. He gave Stuart a big smile as he started to run across

The land of no horizons

the beach.

Lionel and Carrie came and stood next to Stuart.

"Is he a good climber?" Carrie asked.

"Yes, he's very good, but today he's rushing, and that's always very dangerous, especially when your doing an unknown climb."

The bottom of the cliff side was very easy, just large boulders but it changed very quickly to smooth rock, with not many places to get a good grip, the toe holes were very scarce also, but slowly he made his way up towards the shelf.

Russell plotted his path up towards the ledge but there was a problem, with only about ten feet to go there was absolutely nothing to grip too, no hand holes nowhere to put his feet, he was stopped. He couldn't believe his luck, so near yet so far.

All he could do was go back. As he started back down the cliff, he spotted a second route that he could try. This other route would take him away from the ledge, then he would have to go higher than the ledge and finally he might have to jump the last few

The land of no horizons

feet. As he started to climb again he felt a surge of hope. This was a long way round but it looked possible.

The sweat was running down his back as he strained every muscle trying to climb as fast as he could. He was concentrating so much on what he was doing, he didn't notice the breath of fresh air coming from a vent in the rock face, a hole not large but perhaps large enough.

"What's he doing," Lionel said, "he's going away from the ledge?"

"There must be no way across from there, he's trying to find another way," Stuart replied.

"What are the chances that Wolf is still alive?" Carrie asked.

"I was just thinking about that, there's a chance. Reptiles like to eat their food live and some predators will take live food back to their babies," Stuart said.

"I hope you're right and I hope that Russell gets there before that monster gets back," Carrie said

The land of no horizons

Russell was above the ledge but still a few feet away, he could see wolf lying there, covered in blood, not moving. He was close but not close enough. His only chance was to jump. This was something that even he had never done, it was very scarey. To jump from here was almost impossible. He was clinging to a rock face balancing on his toes and thinking of jumping onto a ledge that is only about three feet wide.

The one good thing was that wolf was over on the left side of the ledge and he was to the right. Russell closed his eyes and thought about what he had to do to make this jump. He had come this far, he was not going to give up now. It was possible, he could do it, he told himself. He took a deep breath and using all the strength that he had, he hurled himself towards the shelf.

It took less than a second for his right foot to hit the shelf, when it did it buckled under his weight, this was probably a good thing as his body plummeted forward onto the ledge. Momentum crashed him hard against the back wall of the shelf, he bounced off the wall and off the front of the ledge.

The land of no horizons

Both hands were scrambling for something to grab hold of. His right hand found a lip that he held onto as his body slipped over the edge.

Swinging from a ledge a hundred feet above the English Sea was the most frightening position he had ever been in. His fingers held but only just, his left hand was scratching at the ledge desperately searching for something to hold onto. He found it, a rock imbedded in the shelf but protruding enough that he could get a grip on it. Slowly he pulled himself onto the ledge, first his arms then his body, finally his legs.

As he lay face down desperately trying to catch his breath, he said a silent thank you, to the only one who could be listening. He looked over at Wolf and his heart sank. There was blood covering most of his body, if he was still alive it was only just.

"Wolf, Wolf, can you hear me buddy," he said in a quiet voice.

The puppy didn't move. Russell could feel the tears well up behind his eyes. He reached over and touched him. Did he twitch, he thought that he twitched? Looking closer he thought he saw his chest

The land of no horizons

move, *he's alive, he's alive, he's breathing only just, but he's breathing*. Russell stroked his head gently and said softly into his ear, "I'm sorry I let this happen to you. I'm going to get you down from here, ok."

    Scrambling to his feet he stood up on the shelf and shouted down, "he's alive, he's badly hurt, I'm going to try and make a harness so that I can lower him down to you."

    Stuart gave a jump and punched the air, "he's alive" he said turning to Lionel. "Isn't that great."

    Lionel had a big smile on his face, "he will need treatment, we need to get him down as quickly as possible."

    Stuart turned to Carrie but before he could speak, he could see the tears flowing down her cheek's, "it's ok, he's alive," he said.

    Russell was busy fashioning a harness out of his shirt when a screaming mad pterodactyl appeared just a few feet from his face. The large snout was snapping at him forcing him back against the cave

The land of no horizons

wall. Without a weapon all he could do is cover his face and move back as far as he could.

The pterodactyl screamed so loud Russell thought his eardrums would burst. He had to do something but what, all he had was the rope. Slipping the rope of his shoulders he grabbed it and started to swing it in the direction of the creature that was attacking him. The rope turned out to be an affective weapon. As the pterodactyl attacked, Russell attacked also, he swung the rope towards the massive head that was only a few feet away. Twice he connected, catching his attacker by surprise. The second hit forced the pterodactyl to retreat. It dropped down about twenty feet then it started back towards the ledge.

Russell had loosened the rope so that now he had about ten coils about fifteen feet long. As soon as he saw the face coming towards him, he swung the rope as hard as he could, aiming to catch the flying lizard by surprise.

His strategy worked, again he forced his attacker back. But it was not about to give up, this time it was determined. It came at Russell snapping

The land of no horizons

its long snout. When Russ swung the rope it caught it in its mouth and almost pulled Russell off the shelf.

The tense struggle continued, Russ needed the rope, he could not give it up. The pterodactyl was smart enough to realize that without the rope the man was far less dangerous to him. So it pulled using its mighty wings, trying desperately to pull Russ off the ledge.

Down on the beach, three people watched the deadly battle going on over their heads.

"Is there nothing we can do?" Carrie said.

"I can't think of anything," Stuart said. "The bow will not send an arrow that far. I wish I had gone with him."

"I've got it, Carrie, get the gun, you know where it is?" Lionel said.

"Yes I do," she said excitedly. Then she ran off towards the small cave.

"You have a gun," Stuart said.

"We do, but we have it hidden away, partly because we only have four bullets. It saved us once

The land of no horizons

from the men that live down here. But we hide it away so that no one can steal it."

Carrie came running back waving a pistol around. "Give that to me," Lionel said angrily. "You don't wave a gun around like that, you should know better."

"Sorry daddy."

Lionel gave the gun a quick inspection, then he slipped off the safety catch. Holding the gun in two hands he pointed it in the direction of the ledge.

"Stuart, have you ever fired a gun," he said.

"Yes, why."

"My eyesight is not as good as it used to be, do you think you could take the shot."

"Sure thing professor, give it to me."

Stuart took the gun and aimed it towards the pterodactyl. Holding the gun firmly in both hands, he quietly took aim. He was scared that the ricochet would bounce off the walls and hit Russ but that was a chance that he had to take. Waiting for the right second he gently squeezed the trigger.

Russell out of the corner of his eye, saw Stuart

The land of no horizons

standing on the beach in a peculiar stance. He knew what that stance normally meant but how could that be. Russell sensed what was going to happen, so he flattened himself against the back wall.

The gun exploded in his hand, kicking back hard against his wrist. The noise vibrated throughout the cave, echoing down the main cave and disappearing in the distance. The pterodactyl gave out a loud scream as the bullet passed through its wing hit the roof of the cave and dropped into the sea below. Stunned by the noise of the gun and the bullet ripping through its wing, the flying reptile dropped about forty feet, then it turned away and headed back towards the island.

Russell crashed back against the cave wall as the tension left the rope, he stood there for a second or two to get his breath back. Then he crawled to look over the edge of the ledge, he could see his attacker winging its way towards the island. Looking towards the beach, he gave them a wave to say that he was ok. He crossed the ledge for a quick look at Wolf, he didn't seem to be any worse, his breathing

The land of no horizons

was shallow but he was still breathing.

Gently placing Wolf inside his shirt then tying the ends up so that Wolf could not fall out. This was Russ's simple way to transport Wolf down from the shelf they were on. Slowly Russell lowered the pup down towards the water.

Stuart swam out quickly untied the shirt. Next he placed Wolf on his chest and with a strong back stroke, he swam back to the beach. Lionel raced out and lifted the puppy of Stuart's chest and gently carried him back to their camp.

Carrie was waiting as Lionel brought the puppy to her. She had some warm water ready and she gently washed most of the blood off Wolf. With his Doctor's bag waiting for him, Lionel quickly gave the pup a close examination.

"He doesn't look as bad as I thought he would," Lionel said. "He has lost a lot of blood that's his biggest problem. His skin has been penetrated many times by those sharp teeth. But on the positive side they didn't go in too deep. My biggest worry is that he could come down with some kind of infection. Reptiles are notorious for carrying nasty

The land of no horizons

germs in their mouths, I do have some antibiotics we can try on him."

Lionel dug around in his bag and pulled out a bottle of tablets he took one out and crushed it in his pill crusher. "Now we have to find a way to get some of it into him," he said.

"If we dissolve it in milk, we might be able to get to get him to drink it. But we don't have a baby bottle, we have to think of some other way we get him to drink it?" Carrie said.

"I have some rubber gloves, maybe we can make something out of those."

Russell came running up the beach to where everyone was standing. "How is he?" He asked.

"How are you?" Stuart said. "You scared us all to death, hanging off the ledge like that. Then we thought that thing was going to pull you off, are you ok?"

"I'm ok, but how is Wolf?"

"Daddy said that the wounds could have been worse but his big worry is infection. We are trying to think of a way to get antibiotics into him," Carrie said. "We have some rubber gloves that we think

The land of no horizons

might work but were not sure if they will."

After producing a small box Lionel took out one glove and he held it up so that everyone could see it.

"What if we cut off the big finger, then pierce a small hole in the tip, if we put the crushed tablet into some goat's milk, we might be able to get it down his throat?" Lionel said.

"It's worth a try, I'll go and get the milk," Carrie said, as she hurried away.

"Listen boys?" Lionel said, "I didn't want to say to much in front of Carrie, but Wolf is only just holding onto life. We have to get some milk into him and we have to do it about every four hours. It will be very difficult while he is unconscious but we have to try. If he goes to long without food, well, he will die."

"*I will do whatever it takes just show me what to do,*" Russell said.

"We will all help," Stuart added.

The land of no horizons

CHAPTER NINETEEN

That night Russell woke up every four hours and fed Wolf goats milk. It was not easy, he would give him a few drops then he would wait for them to disappear, then he would give him a few more drops. It would take at least half an hour to feed him the small amount that Lionel had suggested. Then Russell would place Wolf on his bed close to him so that his body warmth would help to keep Wolf warm.

In the morning when Russell woke up Wolf had moved, he was not in the same position as he was when they went to sleep. Was this a good sign, Russell hoped so?

The land of no horizons

It was late morning when Wolf made his first positive movement. All he did was lift his head and open his eye's a little, but everyone took it as a small step in the right direction. He is alive and beating the odds.

Everyone stayed around camp that day just to see how Wolf would do. Mid afternoon, when no one was looking, Wolf woke up. He lifted his head and looked around. Then very slowly he sat up. He moved like a new born deer, everything in slow motion. Finally he managed to get to his feet. Standing there, swaying like a tree in a strong breeze, was the most wonderful thing that could happen. It was Carrie who spotted him first, she then pointed him out to the others. They all watched as he tried to stand, first time he fell back down. The second time he managed to hold himself up for a few seconds. On the third attempt he succeeded.

Russell rushed over and picked him up. He held him close to his face as he fought back the tears.

By the next day it was hard to tell that Wolf had been on death's door. Except for a slight limp,

The land of no horizons

his ordeal with the pterodactyl could have happened weeks ago. He was lapping up milk and eating small pieces of meat. When he lay down on the beach everyone kept a close eye on the sky over the island, they didn't want any more surprise's.

When they were all sat down for their evening meal Russell said, "Professor how come you never told us about the gun?"

"I had almost forgotten about it. Being British I hate guns, I only had it for protection. In some parts of Africa you have to carry one. On the day we got trapped down here I happened to have it with me. It was lucky that I did, that's the second time it has come in handy."

"The second time, when was the first?" Stuart asked.

"It was a long time ago, shortly after we arrived here we had a little run in with the men from the village. We were just getting ourselves set up. We had moved into the cave and built the fence to keep the goats in when one morning we got up and the men were stealing our goats."

The land of no horizons

"At that time I still had the gun close at hand. So I ran into the cave and brought it out. I waved it around but it didn't scare them, they didn't know what it was for. There was a coconut on the table, so I aimed at it, pulled the trigger and as luck would have it I hit it."

"Well, you should have seen them run. The noise was so loud down here it scared the hell out of them and they haven't been back since."

"Shortly after that we hid it away. We only had five bullets when we came here, so with only four bullets left we decided that it should only be used in real emergencies, like the one yesterday."

"I'm happy you had it, it saved my life and Wolf's life too," Russell said

The land of no horizons

CHAPTER TWENTY

The following evening just before they all sat down to eat, a familiar figure stepped out of the jungle and onto the beach. But instead of walking over towards them he stopped on the edge of the jungle.

"Jo Jo come on over," Stuart said. But Jo Jo didn't move. Everyone stopped and looked at him, puzzled by the way he was acting.

"I will go and talk to him," Lionel said. As he strode away heading towards the jungle.

The others all started towards the table again. "What do you think's up with him?" Carrie asked.

The land of no horizons

"I have no idea," Russell replied.

"He's acting strange," Stuart said.

When they reached the table they all sat down, but their eyes never left Jo Jo and Lionel.

It was Jo Jo who was doing all the talking and Lionel just stood there and listened. When Jo Jo stopped talking Lionel looked over towards the table and nodded his head. Then he took Jo Jo's arm and lead him over to the table.

"What's wrong daddy, the way you're acting is making me frightened?"

"As you know Jo Jo left kind of suddenly the last time he was here. The reason behind this was that we saw something and we didn't know what it was. So Jo Jo went to check it out."

"What was it that you saw?" Russell asked.

"We were on the cliff side watching the north village, when Jo Jo spotted, *in the distance,* that some of the trees were dying. He had just come through that area a few days before and he had not seen anything then. So he volunteered to go and have a closer look. I have been watching this area from here and it is getting bigger. The troubling thing is

The land of no horizons

that it seems to be heading this way. Not directly at us, but definitely this way. Now I will let Jo Jo tell you what he saw."

"As the professor said, I was worried about what I thought was happening to those trees but when I got there I was amazed at what I saw. I thought it was locusts' or something like that and in a way I was right. It took about four days to get there. I could hear something before I could see them. I could hear them eating everything insight."

"Ok Jo Jo, tell us what the hell are they?" Russell said sounding very impatient.

"*Ants, giant ants,* not thousands of them but millions of them. And not tiny little ants, but giant ants. They are bright red and about the size of a small spider."

"Red fire ants can be very dangerous," Stuart said. "In South America the ants march for miles, killing small animals and doing lots of damage along the way. That's regular size ants. Can you imagine the damage these ones could do. Also the fire ant bite is very painful, if these are as big as Jo Jo says they are, a couple of bites could be deadly."

The land of no horizons

"It sounds like we have a big problem coming our way, what are we going to do about it?" Carrie asked.

No one spoke for a moment then Russell said, "are we sure that they are coming to this exact place. Or could they bypass us, miss us completely?"

"As you all know" Lionel said, "this valley, within a cave narrows here by the water. It's like a big funnel that ends up here. So if I was gambling man I would say that yes they will end up here on our beach. There is also the grand canal on one side and the lagoon on the other. Again directing them straight at us."

"What about the stream. It will be difficult for them to cross the stream?"Stuart said.

"That's a good point but it will only take one fallen tree that crosses the stream, and they are across," Lionel replied.

"How long do you think it will take them to get here Jo Jo?" Carrie asked.

"Not long, six days, seven at the most"

"That doesn't give us much time, we need to come up with a plan and a good one." Lionel said.

The land of no horizons

They talked as they ate and slowly a plan started to come together. Not a single idea but a multi level plan of attack and defend . The objective was to start the next day, as it was obvious that there was little time to waste.

Once the plan was finalized, the talk changed to tell Jo Jo about how they got that piece of tooth and also explain about how they got the puppy.

The next morning everyone was up early. There was a solemness about the camp. Everyone realized that they had only a short time to implement the plan and then they still had to hope it worked. If it didn't work then there was a good chance that they could all die.

They all agreed, that as a last resort they could try and sail out into the English Sea. This would be a lot of work to get the raft ready in six days. But they had no choice, they had to get it done. The big worry was what if it sank. They didn't know if it would hold all of them, and still float.

The rest of the plan was in small parts, so collecting all the pieces that they needed was top

The land of no horizons

priority. As soon as they finished eating everyone started on their selected jobs. Stuart and Carrie were in charge of getting the vines to bind the logs together. The other three had the task of going out and finding the logs, to build the raft out of. This was a big task as all they had for tools was the camping axe. This was not the ideal tool for chopping down trees.

Carrie and Stuart started off as soon as they had finished their breakfast. The only tool they had was Stuart's Swiss Army Knife. The blade was sharp but it would take time to cut down all the vines that were still needed. They had a few already cut but that would not be enough.

The three men started off into the jungle. To find what they were looking for, this would not be an easy task. They needed long straight logs that they could carry. They had to hope that they were dry enough to float high in the water so that when everyone climbed on, it would still be above water. All these things were questions waiting to be answered.

The next few days passed very quickly.

The land of no horizons

Nothing seemed to work as well as they hoped it would. The raft was taking longer than it should. And all the time the ants were getting closer.

Everyday Lionel took a little time to check on their progress. He would go to one of his vantage points and with the binoculars he could see the path of devastation they were making. When he came back, he confirmed their worst fears, the ants were getting closer faster than they hoped.

"We need to try and deflect them, send them in a different direction," Lionel said.

"And how are we supposed to do that, dad?" Carrie said sounding a little petulant.

"Well, we know that water gives them a problem and also fire gives them a bigger problem. Perhaps we can use one or both of those to slow them down a bit."

"The ants at the moment are on the other side of the stream, what if me and Carrie go to the stream and see if we can stop them from crossing over. They will need something like a fallen log to use as a bridge to get over. If we can get there first and dislodge those bridges, we might be able to stop

The land of no horizons

them or at least slow them down a little."

"It might work," Russell said.

"I don't like it," Lionel said, "it could be dangerous, if you get caught by those ants, well, it could be very dangerous," it seemed like Lionel didn't want to say what he was really thinking.

"We will be ok, daddy," Carrie said as she kissed her dad on the forehead. "If we are going to go, we should go now, so that we can get there before the ants do."

"*Now*, no, that is out of the question, we are about to have our evening meal, it would mean that you will be gone a long time," Lionel said.

"I will look after her, you don't have to worry we will be ok," Stuart said.

Lionel looked flustered, he didn't know what to say. Eventually he said, "ok, but you have to promise me to be careful and not do anything dangerous."

"We'll be all right, we are going to stay on this side of the stream, while they are on the other side," Carrie said.

"Is there anything you need, that will help

The land of no horizons

you?" Russell asked.

"I should take the little folding shovel, my knife and some matches. Other than that I can't think of anything else we might need," Stuart said.

"Ok then, let's get things ready and we will send you on your way," Russell said, as he stood up from the table and headed back to the small cave. Stuart followed while Carrie stayed behind.

"Don't worry dad I will be very careful. You just get that raft ready for when we get back, ok."

"I know you will be ok but you are still my baby and I worry about you."

"I know you worry about me but I'm grown up now and I can look after myself."

Lionel opened his mouth to say something but he thought better of it. He felt that she was going to be alright and he also knew that they needed as much time as possible to get the raft ready.

Stuart and Russell appeared from the small cave, Stuart was carrying the fold-up shovel. "Are you ready?" He asked.

"I'm ready," Carrie said.

"Watch out for those ants they can move very

The land of no horizons

fast," Jo Jo said. "Here, take my spear, it just might come in handy."

"Thanks, Jo Jo," Carrie said as she took the spear from him.

Carrie and Stuart walked out of the camp and just before they entered the jungle they turned around and waved goodbye.

"They'll be ok Lionel, don't worry about them. What we have to worry about is getting that raft seaworthy, all our lives might depend on it," Russell said.

"Your right, they will be fine and yes we have a lot of work to do. Let's get going."

"How far do you think the stream is from here?" Carrie said.

"It's about a mile or so, I guess. That's to the closest part, but what we need to do is go upstream so that we can destroy any natural bridges. Then we can work our way down stream and still stay ahead of them."

"There's a quicker way than taking our usual path and then following the stream. I'll show you this

The land of no horizons

other path, it brings us out just before those little waterfalls."

"Great, you lead the way."

Stuart knew the place that Carrie was talking about, but he didn't know the path. The more he thought about it the happier he was. The stream was quite strong up to those waterfalls, then it splits into two. The majority of the water goes of to the right, with the smaller amount going to the left. The ants would have a very difficult time crossing upstream from the waterfalls. But when they got downstream from the falls, they only had to cross the smaller left arm of the stream. To make things worse it had not rained for five or six days, so the water level on this side would be quite low.

Carrie had found the path that she wanted to show Stuart, and was now in the lead down a path that was obviously not used very much. The jungle seemed quieter than usual, perhaps the animals knew that something bad was coming. Animals could sense trouble and they would just get out of it's way, if they could. For some animals it was as easy as just flying to a different part of the jungle. For others it

The land of no horizons

was not so easy. The giant tortoise might be able to hide in his shell but most animals didn't have anything to hide in. Their only chance was to run and hide and hopefully the danger would pass them by.

Stuart was starting to get tired, they had already had a busy day. Now there was this hike through a thick part of the jungle. Carrie was still leading the way. He liked it when she was in front, he loved to watch her body move, for him it was like poetry in motion. The sway of her hips, the way her shoulders moved, her legs, long and slender. Today she had on the shorts and T shirt that he had given her.

Today would be the first time that they had slept apart from the rest of the group. He had to be careful, he had kissed her once and that had not been greatly received. The last thing that he wanted was to turn her away from him but he wanted her so bad, it hurt.

Time was on his side he kept telling himself. He knew that she was fond of him and she liked to be with him. What he didn't know was if her feeling for him went as deep as his did for her. He was in love

The land of no horizons

with her, madly, deeply. The more time he spent with her the more in love he became. He just wished that she would give him a sign that she felt the same way.

In the distance was a sound, the unmistakable sound of water crashing onto rocks. The waterfalls were close now, only a few hundred feet away. Again he noticed how quiet the jungle was, unnaturally quiet. So quiet it was almost scary.

Carrie had also noticed how quiet things were, at first she had thought that they had scared the animals away. Now that was not the case, something else had brought this hush over the jungle creatures. It was as if they had gone into hiding, knowing that something bad was about to happen.

Was there enough time to do what they needed to do, or would the ants be here before they could accomplish anything? The ants were the biggest threat they had faced since they had been living in this strange land. Could they overcome this threat, or would this be the end for them?

The land of no horizons

CHAPTER TWENTY ONE

Things were better now that Stuart and Russell were here with them. Young men, strong men. But were they strong enough. With everyone relying on them, could they hold everything together.

Carrie couldn't help thinking about Stuart, handsome, charming, funny, vulnerable, Stuart. He means so much to me. If anything happened to him, I don't know what I would do. What are these feelings that I have? He put his body in front of mine, when our lives were threatened by that big cat. He was prepared to die to save my life, and then he kissed me and my reaction was to push him away.

The land of no horizons
What does that mean?

Carrie broke out of the jungle into the clearing that surrounded the waterfalls with Stuart just a step or two behind her. The falls were not running very hard, the water flow was a lot less that Stuart had hoped for. They were stood in the center of the Y part with the majority of the water running away to their right. The smaller stream running off to their left, was only a little more than a trickle. The falls were directly in front of them, and the stream that fed the falls snaked away in the distance curving off to the right. The stream above the falls was not quite as strong as they had expected it to be. The ants would still have a difficult time crossing upstream because the stream was fifteen to twenty feet wide.

"What do you think Stuart?"

"The ants should come down the left side of the main stream and when they get here, with the water level being so low, they should have no trouble finding a way across."

Stuart walked a short distance down the left side of the stream and noticed a line of rocks spanning the stream only inches apart and all of them

The land of no horizons

sticking out of the water.

"Carrie, come here and take a look at this."

"What is it?"

"Look how low the water level is here, these rocks are high and dry, if the ants are as big as we think they are, they will have no problem crossing those rocks."

"Can we fix it some way?"

"The only thing I can think of is to try and dam the other side of the stream and see if we can force some more water this way. We don't have much time, so we have to get a move on if we are going to be successful."

"How do we start."

They walked over to the right side of the stream, to see if it looked possible. This side of the stream was running pretty fast. Just in front of the falls the stream was wide and deep, then it narrowed to about four feet across. But it was still deep. A little further down it widened out a lot, and was only about two feet deep. The bank's on either side of the stream were high all along here.

"This looks like the best spot. We are a little

The land of no horizons

further from the falls than I would have liked but we might be able to make it to work. Those big rocks on the other side will help us. If I can lift them, we will place those first, then we will use smaller rocks to fill in between them. We will do the outsides first, then we will fill in the middle. We will have to build it up almost to the top of the banks, and that will take a lot of time. What do you think, are you up for it?"

Carrie gave him a look, as if to say what do you think I'm doing here. Then she jumped off the bank into the water and started to collect rocks. Stuart took of his runners and followed Carrie into the water.

The big rocks turned out to be heavier than he thought they would. Carrie helped and with the strength of two people, they managed to get four big rocks into the stream. They placed two at each side, this immediately increases the depth of the water. Then they started to fill the gaps between the rocks, but they left the middle open. The water was rushing through the gap at a tremendous speed. Smaller rocks would get washed away in the strong current. It took a few hours to build the sides up to level of the

The land of no horizons

banks. But eventually they got them there.

With only a couple of key rocks left, Stuart stood back to take a look at how things looked. How to get the last two big rocks in place was a problem, a big problem. The water in front of the dam was now over three feet deep. To carry two large rocks through all that fast moving water, was not going to be easy. The only alternative was to come from the down steam side. That would have its own problems, with the water flowing through the hole so fast, it would be almost impossible to place the rocks where they would do the most good.

As Stuart studied the problem, a large rock landed about two feet in front of him, sending a huge plume of water that soaked the few dry bits he still had. When he looked towards Carrie, she had her back to him, trying to dig up another rock.

Stuart could tell from her body language, that she had thrown the rock. So he walked over to the stream bank and scooped up a handful of mud. With a throwing action that sprayed the mud, it hit Carrie on her back leaving a big dirty line all down her back.

The land of no horizons

"Why did you do that?" She screamed. As she jumped to her feet and turned around. It was the big smile on her face that gave her away.

"You know what you did."

She bent down and picked up a big rock and said, "what happened, did a big rock like this one land near your feet and splash you?"

"You know one did because you threw it."

"*Me*, I wouldn't do that to you." All the time she was talking she was moving closer to the stream still carrying the rock.

"Don't splash me with that rock or you will be sorry," Stuart said jokingly.

"*Oh, I will, will I*" She replied, as she threw the rock so it landed a few feet from where Stuart was standing. This second plume of water was smaller than the first one but still sent water all the way up to his head.

"I warned you, now you are going to get it!" Stuart scrambled over to the bank of the stream and crawled out. Carrie screamed and tried to run away but there was nowhere to go, she was trapped. Stuart ran over and picked her up. "You asked for this," he

The land of no horizons

said, as he carried her over to the deep side of the dam.

"Don't you throw me in," she said, as she kicked her legs in a half hearted attempt to escape? Carrie had her arms around Stuart's neck hoping this would stop him from throwing her in.

"Your going in, so you can let go of my neck."

"Oh no I'm not," she said as she tightened her grip.

"You wanna bet." Stuart took two steps back, then he ran and jumped into the water.

Carrie screamed when she realized what he was going to do. But it was too late.

They hit the water and sent up a huge splash. Carrie let go of Stuart's neck as she tried to stand up on the slippy bottom of the stream. "I can't believe you did that," she said, laughing and spitting out water.

"I told you I was going to get you and I did. Are you ok?"

"I'm fine, but I'm soaked to the skin now. Help me out of here you crazy man."

Stuart walked over to the edge of the stream,

The land of no horizons

climbed out and turned around to help out Carrie. He held his hand out so that she could grab hold of it and he would pull her out. She took a tight grip of his outstretched hand and he gently pulled her out of the water. When both of her feet were on dry land, he pulled her again into his arms. He gently held her there and looked into her beautiful blue eyes. She wrapped her arms around him and said, "thank you for saving my life."

"*Saving your life*, you were in no danger that water is only three feet deep."

"No, not then, earlier when that tiger attacked us."

"Even then I didn't, Russ saved us both."

"I know, but you put yourself between me and that monster and that was the bravest thing I have ever seen. With all that was going on, I never got the chance to thank you, so now I have."

"Well, you are very welcome. I guess that now you are in my debt, you owe me one."

"I guess, I do," she said apprehensively.

"Ok, I want to collect now."

"*What.*"

The land of no horizons

"Well you said it, you owe me one and I want it right now. You owe me one kiss. Now I don't mean a little kiss, I mean a proper kiss. One slow kiss."

"You mean it, don't you?"

"Yes I do, one kiss and we are all straight."

"Ok then," she said as she closed her eyes and held her face up.

Stuart gently pulled her closer and placed his lips on hers. The kiss lasted several seconds, before they separated. Carrie's eyes remained closed for a few seconds. When her eyes opened she was looking into his brown eyes.

Neither one spoke for another few seconds then Carrie said, in a soft voice "These clothes are soaking wet," as she separated herself from Stuart and turned away. "Can we build a fire, to try and dry them off?"

Stuart reached out and gently grabbed Carries arm and pulled her back to him. "Listen I'm not sure how to say this but I want to give you this," he said as he took the tooth from around his neck and held it in his hand. "If we were in London, or New York I

The land of no horizons

would take you to a jewelry store and buy you something nice. But we are here in a jungle and the only thing that I have that I can give you is this." He held out his hand, "will you please wear it as a token of our friendship?"

"Russell gave that to you I would feel bad if he was upset because you gave it to me."

"Don't worry about that, I told him that I wanted to give it to you and he said that I could do whatever I wanted with it." Stuart let the tooth hang on the leather necklace then he slipped it over her head. Carrie flipped her hair out of the way and the tooth settled on her chest.

"Thank you Stuart, that's very sweet of you, I will treasure it forever." She reached up and kissed him gently on the lips, pulling back, she again looked deeply into his eyes. Stuart you are a very special friend and I need you to be that friend and just a friend. I love you as a friend can we leave it at that for now."

Stuart shrugged his shoulders and said, "if that's what you want then that's the way it will be."

"Good now will you make a fire so that I can

The land of no horizons

dry off these clothes. Can we do that?"

"We can if the matches are still dry," he said, as he dug into his pocket trying to find the matches.

"They look ok," he said as he inspected the waterproof packet.

"Good I will go and find some wood to burn." Carrie quickly crossed the left side of the stream, and disappeared into the bush.

Stuart was baffled by the way Carrie acted. He knew she liked him, he thought she liked the kiss but then to just walk away the way she did. It was a little strange but at least she said that she loved him, and that put a big smile on his face.

Stuart looked around for twigs to use as kindling and anything else he could find to help the fire get going. He found a bunch of dry leaves and some twigs. Just what he needed to get the fire started.

The smoke was quite thick as the leaves burned, soon the twigs were burning. Carrie still hadn't come back. Stuart collected some larger twigs and dropped them on the fire. He was just about to go and look for Carrie when she appeared carrying a

The land of no horizons

huge armful of twigs and broken branches.

"Are you ok, I was just thinking about coming to look for you?"

"Why wouldn't I be ok, I have lived down here for a long time and I can look after myself?"

"I know you can. Here let me take some of that wood from you."

"No that's ok, I have it," she said, as she waded through the shallow water. When she got close to the fire, she let the whole bundle drop.

"Can you build up the fire while I go and wash this top, it's dirty from all the wood?"

Carrie removed the T shirt she was wearing to reveal the animal skin top that she wore. When she reached the stream she knelt down and started to scrub the shirt.

Stuart took off his shirt and spread it out on a bush, that was close to the fire. When Carrie came back to the fire, she did the same. Then she sat down next to Stuart.

"When we get out of here, do you think you could show me some of America?"

"Of course, I'd love to show it to you. There

The land of no horizons

are lots of great places to see."

"What's you favorite place in all of North America?"

"I have lots of places I like, my favorite city is New York."

"Tell me about New York."

Stuart started to talk about one of the greatest city's in the world. He started with Central Park and Madison Avenue. Then he talked about the shops he would take her to. After a few minutes he looked around at her and she was fast asleep. He smiled put some more wood on the fire and lay down next to her and fell asleep.

It was Carrie moving around that awoke him. She must have been up for a while because she had some food waiting for him.

"Good, your awake, I was just going to wake you, we don't have a lot of time the ants are closer than we thought."

"Have you seen them?"

"Yes, the first ones are about half a mile down the path. They are moving a lot quicker than I

The land of no horizons

thought they would. I expect that they will be here in about an hour, maybe less."

"That soon, eh."

"And we have another problem, the water flow coming over the falls is down. So is the water going down left-hand side of the stream. We have to get those other rocks in quickly, or we are in trouble, big trouble."

"Ok, let's do it now."

Stuart had already rolled the last two big rocks over to the far bank, they just needed to be put in place.

Both Stuart and Carrie jumped into the shallow side of the dam. On reaching the other side they grabbed hold of the larger of the two rocks. With a great deal of difficulty they managed to carry it to the center of the dam.

"We only have one chance to get this in place. We need to swing it and then let it go at the same time. If we are lucky, it will fall through the hole and land at the bottom. Are you ready?"

"I'm ready do it quick before I drop it."

"Ok, on three, one, two, three."

The land of no horizons

They swung the rock back and forward and on three they let it go. It more fell forward than was thrown but when it settled it had plugged the bottom part of the hole in the dam.

"Nice work Carrie, that is just about perfect. The next one is smaller, but we have to try and get it to sit on top of that one. That will be tricky."

"You can bet it will with all that water flowing through that hole, it will be very tricky."

"We have to try, the higher the water level on the other side the better chance we have of heading the ants in another direction."

"Ok, let's do it, we can't get any wetter."

This rock was not as heavy as the first one, but it was still heavy enough that they had to be very carful not to drop it on themselves. Stuart walked backwards, with Carrie taking a good share of the weight. When they got to the center of the steam, they followed the same procedure as last time. This time it was not so successful. When the rock hit the fast flowing water, the water pushed the rock from where it was supposed to sit. Now it was sitting behind the first rock, doing no good at all.

The land of no horizons

"That didn't work," Carrie said.

"No, it didn't."

"Let's see if we can lift it into place."

Carrie gave a look that said *I don't think it will.* But she took her place ready to lift the rock. *This is going to be almost impossible,* she thought.

"Shall we try it on three?" Stuart said.

"Ok"

"One, two, three."

They both lifted with all their strength and slowly the rock came up. The weight of the rock plus the water flow hitting them in the face, made this harder to do than the first rock. But slowly the rock slipped into place. Stuart was using every once of strength that he had and Carrie was putting everything she had into getting that rock into place. With one final push the rock sat where they wanted it to. Slowly they backed away hoping that it would stay put and it did.

"We did it," Stuart said.

"Only just, if it hadn't gone in when it did I would have dropped it."

"I know what you mean, I was just about dead

The land of no horizons

when it fell into place. Let's see if we are getting enough water flowing down the other side?"

Stuart was out first and he offered to help Carrie out but this time she preferred to climb out on her own. When Carrie got to where Stuart was standing he had a smile of satisfaction on his face.

"We did it Carrie, we did it."

"*Yes*, we did."

There was now lots of water flowing down this side of the stream now, all the rocks that were sticking out of the water before were now covered by at least four inches of fast flowing water.

"Lets hope this is enough to keep the ants on that side of the stream." She had only just stopped speaking when there was an unusual sound in the distance. It was a sound like nothing they had heard before. It sounded like an army marching in big boots. But this army was not marching in step, it was *one* noise coming closer by the second.

Carrie and Stuart just stood and waited. At first it was hard to tell what was coming down that path, then it was like a river of blood as the red ants came clearly into view. The ants were following the stream

The land of no horizons

down towards the falls.

As the lead ants got past the falls and down to the stream they climbed down the bank to the waters edge, then they stopped. It was as if they expected to cross here and they couldn't understand why there was so much water.

The waves of ants kept coming, spilling past the first ones to arrive and were soon a hundred feet downstream, all on the bank looking at the water. In the distance there was no end, the ants just kept coming.

Stuart and Carrie didn't speak, they just watched the ants. They were big, as big as a smaller tarantula. Their color was amazing, brilliant red, as red as a fire truck or a London bus.

Every ant stopped moving, the sea of red was motionless. All that the front ones did, was look at the water. Then as if someone had told them to move, they did, all together. Now the ants that were furthest down stream were now the leaders and all the others followed them.

"Oh my god," Carrie said, "we were so concerned about the water here we forgot about what

The land of no horizons

was downstream. All it will take is one branch across the water and all the work we did will be for nothing."

Stuart grabbed his shirt, spade, and Jo Jo's spear, then he looked around for Carrie, she was already running in the same direction as the ants. Stuart started after her.

It took a few minutes to pass the front ants, they were going at a fast pace. It was difficult for Carrie and Stuart because there was no path on this side of the stream. Sometimes they could run on the bank of the stream, but most of the time they had to run in the water. This was very tiring and much slower. Carrie almost fell twice after tripping over hidden rocks.

The first bridge that the ants could use was not much more than a twig and Carrie cleared that away easily. The next one was a bigger problem. It was a large piece of tree that had obviously been there for many years. It spanned the stream in a narrow spot, just before the stream widened out to about eight feet.

At first glance they thought that this was

The land of no horizons

impossible. A large piece of tree like this was too heavy for them. Stuart strode through the stream and pushed hard on the tree. He was surprised when the tree moved.

"Come and give me a hand, I think we might be able to move this," he said.

Carrie had seen the tree move and she was already moving through the water to see if she could help.

"This looks like a big tree for us to move."

"I know, but I think, if we can rock it, we might be able to get it to fall into the stream. Are you ready to give it a try?"

"I'm here, let's do it before the ants get here."

They both took up positions on the side where the ants would come from and started to rock the big log. At first there was almost no movement. But slowly as they got a rhythm going, the log began to move. Each push gave them hope that they could dislodge the log and drop it into the water.

The ants were closing in and this made them push all that much more. They pushed using every bit of strength they had, and yet it still needed more.

The land of no horizons

Finally just as the ants came into view the log slid off the bank and fell into the water. Carrie collapsed into the water, tired beyond anything she had ever known.

Stuart looked at the log and his heart sank. Yes it had fallen off the bank, but it was still reachable by the ants. In desperation he walked over to the log and grabbed hold of it and lifted. The way the log had landed it was perched on a rock and the weight must have been similar on both sides. When Stuart lifted the log, it came up and he managed half a step before he dropped it down again. The half step was enough to get it away from the edge and into deeper water.

Carrie had regained some of her strength and she came over to Stuart and said, "great job Tarzan, now let's get going there will be other trees to move."

Stuart gave a noticeable groan as he slowly got to his feet. The ants were now only a few feet behind them and showing no sign of slowing down. Carrie was a short distance away as Stuart started after her. They both got to the bank of the stream about the same time. In this area the bank on this side of the stream was quite high, and the soil very loose. It was

The land of no horizons

with great difficulty that they managed to scramble out of the water and onto dry land.

Tired as they were, they took a few seconds to recover from the struggle that they had just been through. When they checked on the ants, they were stopped again, looking at the water.

"Let's get going, we need to check the rest of the stream while we still can," Stuart said.

Carrie slowly got to her feet, took a deep breath and said, "I'm right behind you."

Stuart was just about to leave the small clearing, when Carrie's voice stopped him.

"Stuart......come here......and look at this."

"What," he said, as he turned back to see Carrie stood watching the ants.

"Come here," she was waving her hand for him to go back to where they had been standing.

When he got there, he couldn't believe what he was seeing. All the ants were motionless except at the back, where some of the ants had cut large leaves from one of the plants. They were now passing those leaves over their heads from one ant to another. When the leaf got to the front, the ants laid it on the

The land of no horizons

water. Then three ants climbed on it and let the current take them across the stream.

Stuart and Carrie just stood there in amazement. The ants couldn't find a bridge so they used leaves as boats! There was no way to stop them. Now instead of a sea of red all they could see were leaves, hundreds of leaves, all heading for the stream. Soon there would be hundred's of ants crossing the stream and there was nothing they could do about it. Stuart picked up some rocks and threw them at the leaves. This was more an act of frustration than a serious attempt to sink all the leaves.

"Let's get going," Carrie said in a low voice. "We have to get back to camp and warn the others."

Stuart threw his last rock and started after her.

The land of no horizons

CHAPTER TWENTY TWO

When Carrie and Stuart stepped out of the bush that surrounds the camp they hardly recognized the place. There was a line of branches and twigs running the whole length of the beach.

"They probably plan to set them on fire, *if*, I mean *when* the ants get here," Stuart said.

Carrie didn't reply she just walked over to the barricade stepped over it and walked over towards the cave. The pen that held the goats was empty. All three men were on the beach working on the raft. They were so consumed with what they were doing they didn't see them coming. Only when they got

The land of no horizons

almost to where they were working, that Lionel spotted them.

It was Russ that spoke first, "how are you guys?" He asked.

"We're ok, but I hope you're ready the ants will be here in about half an hour."

"That quick, eh." Lionel said. "We are almost ready, we need your help to get the raft in the water."

"Good, so it is ready?" Stuart said.

"We haven't managed to get it in the water yet so we are not positive it will float. Come on over and take a look," Russell said.

The raft looked good, it was obviously quickly put together but it looked sturdy. They had put a mast in the middle and there was a piece sticking out from the back for someone to sit on, to try and steer from. There were three long straight poles and three pieces of wood that looked like they were supposed to be paddles. The whole raft did look heavy, would it float that was the question?

"The raft looks great guys, but it looks heavy. We need to try it, those ants will be here very soon," Stuart said.

The land of no horizons

"You're sure they are coming this way? Jo Jo asked.

"Positive," Carrie said.

Everyone looked a little despondent, then without another word they all started towards the raft.

The raft was as heavy as it looked but with all five of them lifting they managed to lift it clear of the ground and they all managed to stand straight. Russell and Jo Jo were at the front as they were the tallest. Stuart was on one back corner with Lionel on the other. Carrie was in the middle of the back lifting with all her strength.

The raft had been built only about ten feet from the water edge, but those ten feet were some of the most strenuous ten feet any of them had ever walked. When Russ and Jo Jo got in deep enough that the water came up to their knees, everyone lowered the raft onto the water.

To everyone's amazement it floated. The right side was a bit higher than the left but it floated. And it floated quite high.

Russell was the first to jump on board. Then

The land of no horizons

Lionel clambered on board. Stuart helped Carrie to climb on, then he followed. Jo Jo was the last. Even with them all on the raft kept afloat, it was now low in the water but high enough that they didn't get their feet wet.

"We need to have three people on the right hand side so it balances out better but other than that we seem to be ok, agreed" Lionel said.

They all nodded in agreement.

"Good, with a bit of luck we should be able to make the island but only if we have to. The only other thing we have is the barricade, we just have to hope it stops them. Ants are known for not being the smartest creatures, lets hope they walk into fire like they are supposed too," Lionel said.

"Are you planning on taking some supplies with us?" Stuart asked.

"Well not really, all we planned on taking was one of our long pieces of nylon rope, and the few tools that we have," Russell said.

"Lets pull the raft up onto the beach and hope we don't have to use it," Lionel said.

They all jumped off the raft and they pushed it

The land of no horizons

so it caught on the sand. Stuart and Russell headed towards the cave to collect the things they wanted to take with them. Carrie stayed and talked to her dad as Jo Jo worked on some torches so that they could start the barricade on fire. Jo Jo was painting some thick gooey stuff onto one end of the torches, this was a sap from one of the trees that flourishes down here. The sap burned very slowly, so the torches would burn for hours.

Wolf, who had been sleeping on the beach all this time, suddenly he woke up and started to look around, it was as if something had disturbed his sleep. He snuggled down again, he didn't seem to have a care in the world.

"Was everything ok while you were gone?" Lionel asked.

"Of course daddy, what did you expect?"

"You never know, it can be very dangerous in this place, there are many perils that can befall a young girl like yourself."

"Dad, I'm not a baby anymore. Plus Stuart was there, he would look after me."

"I know that Stuart is a fine young man but he

The land of no horizons

has eyes for you and you have not had a lot of practice with boys. So I want you to be very careful around him, ok my dear."

"Yes daddy, *I will be careful,* but don't worry I can handle Stuart."

Lionel was not so sure, he had seen the way that Stuart looked at Carrie, was it love or lust, if only he knew for sure.

Wolf got up shook the sand out of his coat and looked towards the jungle. Something was not right he could feel it, he looked for Russell, he was not there. He took one more look around, then he went to look for Russell.

Carrie looked around and noticed that Jo Jo was nowhere to be seen, "where's Jo Jo, dad?" she asked.

"I don't know, he was by the raft the last time that I saw him."

"Do you think he went to check on the ants, they should be here any minute now?"

"He could have. But don't worry about him he can look after himself, let's see what the boys are up to. Perhaps they need a hand."

The land of no horizons

Just as Lionel said that, the boys appeared from the cave. Stuart had a long length of yellow climbing rope while Russell carried the small axe and the shovel. Before the boys got back to the raft, Jo Jo came rushing into view.

"We only have a few minutes" he said, "the ants are right behind me."

"Ok everyone, get a torch and light it," Lionel said. "Then spread out along the fire break. We all need to light it about the same time, we will only have a few seconds from when the ants enter the clearing to being up to the fire break. Please everyone be very careful we don't know how poisonous these little monsters are."

Jo Jo handed out the torches as Russell lit a match. All the torches had the flammable sap on them, as soon as the match touched the sap it sprang into flames.

Wolf's bark was the first indication that the ants were closing in. He couldn't see them but he knew they were there and he let out a bark to warn everyone.

Jo Jo with his long strides walked quickly over

The land of no horizons

to the far side of the cove that they lived in. Carrie took the middle position, with Lionel on her left and Russell on her right. Stuart took the far right side of the fire break, each one held their torch at the ready, waiting, listening.

The ants broke out of the jungle with no warning, when they hit the beach they seemed to run towards the barricade. Carrie was the first one to light the branches and twigs that made up the fire brake. Fire leapt from the dry sticks as she moved slowly towards her dad, touching the dry branches as she went. Lionel was doing the same as he closed the gap between him and Carrie. All the others men were doing the same thing, lighting their section of barricade.

The ants seemed to be in a hurry, when they got to the fire they tried to run through it. The crackling sound of ants burning up in the fire was unsettling. They just kept on coming, wave after wave, thousands, maybe hundreds of thousands.

The first drop of rain landed on Carrie's nose, she looked up at the huge dome that covered most of the cave. To her horror it was full of dark swirling

The land of no horizons

clouds, she knew what that meant, rain, and lots of it.

"Look up everyone," she said.

All eyes turned to look at the great dome.

"Its going to rain, isn't it?" Stuart said.

"Yes, and hard, very hard," Lionel replied.

"Should we get on the raft just in case it puts the fire out." Russell said.

It was at that second that it started to pour, the rain was so hard that it was hard to speak or breath. They were all soaked to the skin within seconds. The fire was blazing away one second and the next it was just a hissing smoldering mess.

"Move now," Russell screamed. "Everyone to the raft."

Without a second word they all rushed towards the raft. It was Russ who got there first he pushed it clear of the sand then held the raft steady, so that everyone could get on, then finally he climbed on himself. With a push the raft moved slowly away from the beach. They all relaxed a little as the gap between them and the beach grew wider.

Carrie was the first one to notice that wolf was not there.

The land of no horizons
"Where's Wolf?" She yelled.

"Oh no," Russell said from the front of the raft, "where is he can you see him?"

The rain was so hard, that it was difficult to see even that short of a distance.

"There he is," Jo Jo yelled, trying to be heard over the rain. "I'll get him." He jumped off the raft and disappeared under the water, when he surfaced he started to swim towards the shore.

"Grab a paddle and let's see if we can get closer to the beach," Carrie said. The three paddles were picked up with only Russell not having one. Russ stood holding the mast desperately trying to see Wolf through the driving rain.

Jo Jo was almost back at the beach when wolf ran off. Russell didn't hesitate he took one large step and dove into the water. Ten feet from the raft he surfaced and with a strong stoke he swam towards the beach.

The rain was still coming down like a monsoon as Russell hit the beach. Jo Jo appeared as if out of nowhere, and even from the raft they could see at least six ants on him. In his arms he had hold of

The land of no horizons

Wolf. Reaching out with his long arms he passed the puppy to Russ and at the same time he let out a terrible scream. The slim body collapsed into the water. Russell grabbed him by his ragged shirt with his right hand, and started back towards the raft.

Stuart reacted immediately, diving into the rough water coming up a short distance from the two men.

"Take Wolf and I'll bring Jo Jo," Russell said.

Stuart did as he was told and he swam back to raft with the dog. Russell used his life guard training to flip Jo Jo over and swim towards the raft. The pain on the tall black mans face was intense, his eyes were closed tight. His face was clenched as if he was in agony.

With the dog safely in Carrie's arms the brothers tried desperately to get Jo Jo onto the raft. With Lionel and Carrie pulling on his arms and the boys trying to get underneath to give some lift, it was still a struggle.

"One more push, guys," Carrie yelled, "we almost have him."

With all their strength the boys pushed and at

The land of no horizons

the same time Lionel and Carrie pulled. With the strength and determination of four people all working together they succeeded. Jo Jo was safely on the raft.

"How is he, daddy?"

"That's hard to tell. His leg is starting to swell, it doesn't look good that's for sure. I can only see one bite mark, which is good. If he's this bad after one, can you imagine how he would be after two or three?"

"He would be dead wouldn't he, daddy?"

No one answered that question, no one needed too.

"Is there anything we can do, professor?" Russell asked.

"No, not really. I think I will put a tourniquet on his leg, this should slow down the poison from traveling to his organs. Hopefully this will give the poison enough time to disperse out of his system, without doing any permanent damage."

"You look after him and we will try and get us over to the island, if we can?" Stuart said.

The rain was starting to slow down a little. It

The land of no horizons

was still raining hard, but less than the torrents of rain of a few minutes ago. Looking at the beach was scary, it was a bright red color from one end to the other. Russell passed out the paddles and they started to paddle towards the island. There was no rush, the raft was staying afloat and the ants were on the beach. They were safe, for now.

Paddling was hard, the raft was not easy to guide and it didn't go very fast. They had only traveled a short distance when the rain slowed to a heavy drizzle. It was Carrie that looked back towards the beach. She was half expecting to see what she saw. It still scared the hell out of her.

"Hey, look at the beach," she said.

Everyone immediately looked towards the beach.

"What are they doing?" Russell asked.

"They are using leaves to float on. They did the same thing when they crossed the stream," Carrie replied.

"You've got to be kidding me!" Russell exclaimed. "Where do they get the brains to do that?"

The land of no horizons

"I don't know but we are ahead of them, and we need to stay that way," Stuart said.

Lionel was keeping a close eye on Jo Jo. Every few minutes he loosened the turnkey around his leg, to let the blood flow through. It seemed to be working, Jo Jo was no worse and he might even be a little better. His face was more relaxed, the pain seemed to have slipped from his body. Hopefully this was all a good sign.

Looking back towards the beach, Carrie felt her uneasiness increase again. There were now hundreds of leaves in the water, all with three or four ants on them.

"Are they getting closer?" Carrie said.

"No, they can't be," Stuart said, not sounding too sure that what he was saying was true.

"You know what, I think they are getting closer. But how can they do that? Russell said.

"I think they're paddling, I think that they are using their legs to paddle. They must be because they are catching up to us." Carrie replied.

There was now no doubt the ants were definitely closer and getting closer by the second.

The land of no horizons

Lionel was still watching Jo Jo, so the other three started to paddle harder. At first they had no rhythm, they were all paddling but not together.

"We all need to paddle at the same time," Russell said.

"Ok," Carrie said, looking to Russell to take the lead.

Stuart fell in with the other two and soon the raft was moving much smoother, the strokes were now much more fluid. The raft was only just staying ahead of the ants.

The sea behind them was a mixture of green and red, there were only a few ants left on the beach.

"If we get to the island first the ants will be just behind us. We will be stepping into the unknown, none of us have ever been to the island before. We don't know what to expect," Lionel said.

"Your right dad, what are you thinking."

"I was wondering, if we shouldn't just try and move out of their way. It looks to me that they are heading for the island, if we move over and head towards the cliffs they might just go past us?"

"That's a gamble professor we would be giving

The land of no horizons

up the slight head start that we have, what do you guys think? Russell asked.

"I think that he has a good point, the ants are not after us, we are just in their way. If we move out of their way, they might just keep going towards the island," Stuart said.

"I agree, why would the ants be after us, we haven't done anything to them," Carrie said.

Looking back, the ants had spread out. They covered a large area, it would take a lot of hard paddling to get out of their way but it was possible.

Stuart was on the log that stuck out from the back of the raft. He started to paddle harder on his right side trying to make the raft turn to his left. Carrie was on the right side so she also paddled harder. Russell eased up slightly on his paddling and slowly the raft turned to the left and headed closer to the cliffs.

Lionel had moved over to the right-hand side of the raft and using just his hands, he was also paddling. Even Jo Jo was paddling as best that he could, he was still in pain but he was improving rapidly.

The land of no horizons

Slowly it seemed to be working, the ants didn't seem to want to chase them, it was the island that they wanted to get to. The rain had continued to ease up slightly but it was still raining.

The raft gave a noticeable shudder as if they had hit something. Then it started to move quicker. Wolf barked, he could feel that something was wrong. The raft was moving on its own, no one was paddling. A current was pushing them towards the cliffs.

When the raft was about ten feet from the cliff side, the current started to pull them away.

"What's happening?" Carrie said in a very frightened voice.

No one spoke, until Lionel yelled, "whirlpool! We are in a whirlpool."

It was hard to tell at first it looked just like an underwater current was dragging the raft along. But soon it started to take shape, the water was spinning, getting more defined all the time.

"We have to get out of this in a hurry or it will suck us right down the middle," Lionel said. " I've seen this before it gets very powerful, we have only

The land of no horizons

a few minutes or it will be too late."

"I have an idea," Russell said. "Try and keep us to the outside edge for as long as you can." Russell grabbed the climbing rope that they had brought with them and started to work on it. Everyone else went to the left side of the raft and started to paddle as hard as they could. The whirlpool was gaining momentum, the water spinning faster and the center was getting deeper.

Russell had made a rough lasso. The raft was just coming round to the cliff's again. There was an outcrop of rock that if he could get the rope onto, might hold them. There was no point in twirling it over his head he had never thrown a lasso in his life. His hope was to throw the rope over the rock and hope that it held.

Just before they got level with the rock he hoped to lasso, he tossed the rope and missed. He dragged in the rope as fast as he could and threw it again. It missed again.

"Let me try" Jo Jo said, "I'm taller and I have longer arms I might get lucky."

"Russell passed over the rope and took a

The land of no horizons

position next to Stuart and started to paddle as hard as he could. The cliff face was coming up faster this time and the raft was starting to lean steeply into the whirlpool. Jo Jo was trying to balance himself, he only had one good leg to try and balance on. He waited until the very last second, then with his long reach he leaned out and flipped the rope over the rock. He pulled on the rope and the nose tightened.

"You did it," Russell yelled. "Now let the rope go lose and when we get close the next time around, we all need to pull on the rope and try and pull us out of here."

Jo Jo wrapped the rope once around the center mast. All the time that they were getting closer to the cliff, he took the slack out of the rope.

"Before we get close to the cliff we need to start pulling, ok" Russell said. "This might be our one and only chance, let's get it right."

With the power of the whirlpool growing, they all tensed at the task ahead of them. Could they pull the raft and themselves clear of this deadly whirlpool? The ants were still a danger to them, the whirlpool was sucking them towards the raft, not just

The land of no horizons

one, but hundreds of them.

"Now" Russell yelled, and they all except Jo Jo, started to pull on the rope. Jo Jo was sitting by the mast taking the slack out of the rope, as he did he wound it around the mast. The first part was quite easy as they moved towards the cliff, but when the current tried to pull them away it was very different. The rope went taught and the raft stopped but it stayed in the whirlpool. The mast bent under the strain, it was not built to hold the raft like this.

"We have to pull harder," Russell said.

They all pulled as hard as they could and their success was minimal. They might have gained a couple of inches that's all.

"Again, *pull*," he yelled.

They all strained every muscle they had, again they gained a couple of inches.

"Do it like your life depends on it, *pull*."

This time they seemed to have a little more success they gained about a foot or two. They were still about ten to twelve feet from the cliff but they were closer to the top of the whirlpool. If they could get a few feet more they would be on the crest, and

The land of no horizons

hopefully then the pull of the whirlpool would ease enough that they could climb onto the rocks.

"Ok, are you ready, let's do it one more time" Russell yelled.

"*Ants,*" Carrie yelled. "On the raft."

They all turned to look, a couple of ants had made their way onto the raft. Their leaf must have got caught against the raft and they climbed on board. Wolf was the first one to react he ran over grabbed one in his mouth and shook it as hard as he could. When he dropped it, the ant quivered a little then it slid into the water. Jo Jo killed the other one with one of the long poles. He managed to hit it twice with the pole, then it followed the fist one into the water.

The whirlpool was now going very fast. The raft was at a steep angle, making the job of pulling it clear all the harder. Also the mast looked like it was ready to pull out of the hole that it sat in. When they built the raft they used vine both on top and underneath, to hold the mast in place. They never expected that the mast would be called upon to hold the raft against such relentless pressure.

The land of no horizons

"Lets try again, ready *pull hard*," Russell yelled. This time the raft moved a couple of feet, so that it was almost to the crest of the whirlpool.

"We did good," Lionel shouted, trying to be heard over the noise the swirling water made. "One more time, pull," the raft leveled out as it cleared the crest.

"The mast is coming out, we have to get off the raft now," Jo Jo screamed.

"Our only hope is the rope, we have to use the rope to pull ourselves onto the rocks," Stuart said. " Carrie you go first you're the lightest."

"No let someone else go first."

"Carrie you go first," Lionel said in a stern voice.

She knew that voice well and what it meant. She grabbed hold of the rope, took one look back and jumped into the water. The cliff was only about five feet in front of her but she had a terrible time getting closer. Dragging herself with one hand then the other, she inched her way towards the rocks.

"Will you go next Stuart, then you can help me if I need it?" Lionel asked.

The land of no horizons

There didn't seem to be anything to say to that request, so he looked at his brother who nodded his approval. Grabbing the rope he moved close to the edge of the raft and took a huge leap. He almost lost his grip on the rope when he hit the water but when he surfaced he was only a foot or so behind Carrie. The tiredness was etched on Carrie's face, she was having difficulty hanging on to the rope in the rough water.

"Let me help you," Stuart said, as he wrapped his arm around her waist. Kicking as hard as he could and pulling on the rope with his other arm, they closed in on the rocks that meant safety. With one foot in a good toe hold and both hands free to grab the rocks Carrie pulled herself clear of the water and finally onto the rocks. Stuart was still knee deep in the water waiting for the professor.

"You next professor," Stuart shouted.

Lionel stood on the end of the raft, hesitated for a second, then he took a mighty leap. Stuart grabbed Lionel and pulled him so that his head was out of the water. Pushing him towards the place where Carrie had climbed out Lionel slowly dragged

The land of no horizons

himself out of the water.

Just as Lionel was clambering onto the rocks there was a loud cracking sound from the raft. Stuart looked back just in time to see the mast fly from the raft and the raft disappear into the ibis of the whirlpool. Russell and Jo Jo were hanging onto the rope as they vanished out of sight.

"*RUSS*," Stuart screamed in anguish. The rope was still tense as he pulled on it. "Professor, haul in the rope."

Carrie jumped up and tried to pull in the rope, but it was too hard for her. Lionel grabbed hold and the two of them started to pull on it as hard as they could but they weren't making any headway. Stuart found a good foothold even though he was still in the water. He pulled on the rope with every ounce of strength he had.

Slowly, ever so slowly they pulled the rope in. Russell's head popped over the crest of the whirlpool and this gave them renewed strength. All three of them pulling in unison managed to get Russell to the rocks. Jo Jo was still hanging on to the rope, for his life did depend on it. With Russell on the rocks the

The land of no horizons

rope was lighter and they managed to get Jo Jo safely onto the rocks. Finally Stuart pulled himself out of the water.

"Wolf, where is Wolf?" Carrie cried. She had been so busy that she hadn't noticed the big bulge in Russell's shirt.

"Don't worry he's ok," Russell said as he pulled his shirt out of his shorts and the puppy rolled out onto the rocks. "I had just stuck him under my shirt when the mast went, luckily he stayed there or we would have lost him."

Jo Jo leaned over and shook Stuart's hand and without saying a word he shook everyone's hand in turn. They all leaned back against the hard rocks, tired, wet, but happy to be alive.

The land of no horizons

CHAPTER TWENTY THREE

Three days had passed since the whirlpool incident, life was getting back to normal. They had sat on those rocks for a couple of hours, then just as suddenly as the whirlpool arrived it went away. The ants were all gone, the whirlpool consumed them all. Which started the question, did the ants know that the whirlpool was coming? If so was this some kind of mass suicide? Everyone had there own opinion, but it would be one of those questions, that would never have an answer.

It was a long swim back to their beach. Russell being the best swimmer stayed close to Lionel to

The land of no horizons

make sure that he was ok. He also swam all the way back doing the backstroke, because he had Wolf on his chest.

They had lost the raft, and the spade, plus the axe, but the axe for some reason was designed to float. And float it did, a few days later while they were fishing, Carrie saw the axe floating a short distance from the beach she swam out and retrieved it. This is a one of their most useful tools and they were happy to get it back.

Cleaning up the beach, and rounding up the goats had taken a couple of days, but now things had settled back down to normal again. Jo Jo had gone hunting, Stuart and Carrie were off somewhere collecting fruit or they might have gone to do some fishing. Lionel was pottering around doing something, but nobody knew what.

Russell was just sitting on a large rock throwing a stick for Wolf to retrieve. Wolf was back to being a healthy puppy again. He showed no signs of problems from his near death experience. He was eating pieces of meat and growing like a puppy of his age should.

The land of no horizons

As Russell was sitting there relaxing, a bit of a song came into his head and he started to sing.

"This is my life
this is my life
this is my life
my life.
This is my life
this is my life
this is my life
my life..........

ISBN 1425185495-5